TIL THERE WAS YOU

A MISFIT INN NOVELLA

KAIT NOLAN

Til There Was You

Written and published by Kait Nolan

Copyright 2020 Kait Nolan

Cover design by Lori Jackson

AUTHOR'S NOTE: The following is a work of fiction. All people, places, and events are purely products of the author's imagination. Any resemblance to actual people, places, or events is entirely coincidental.

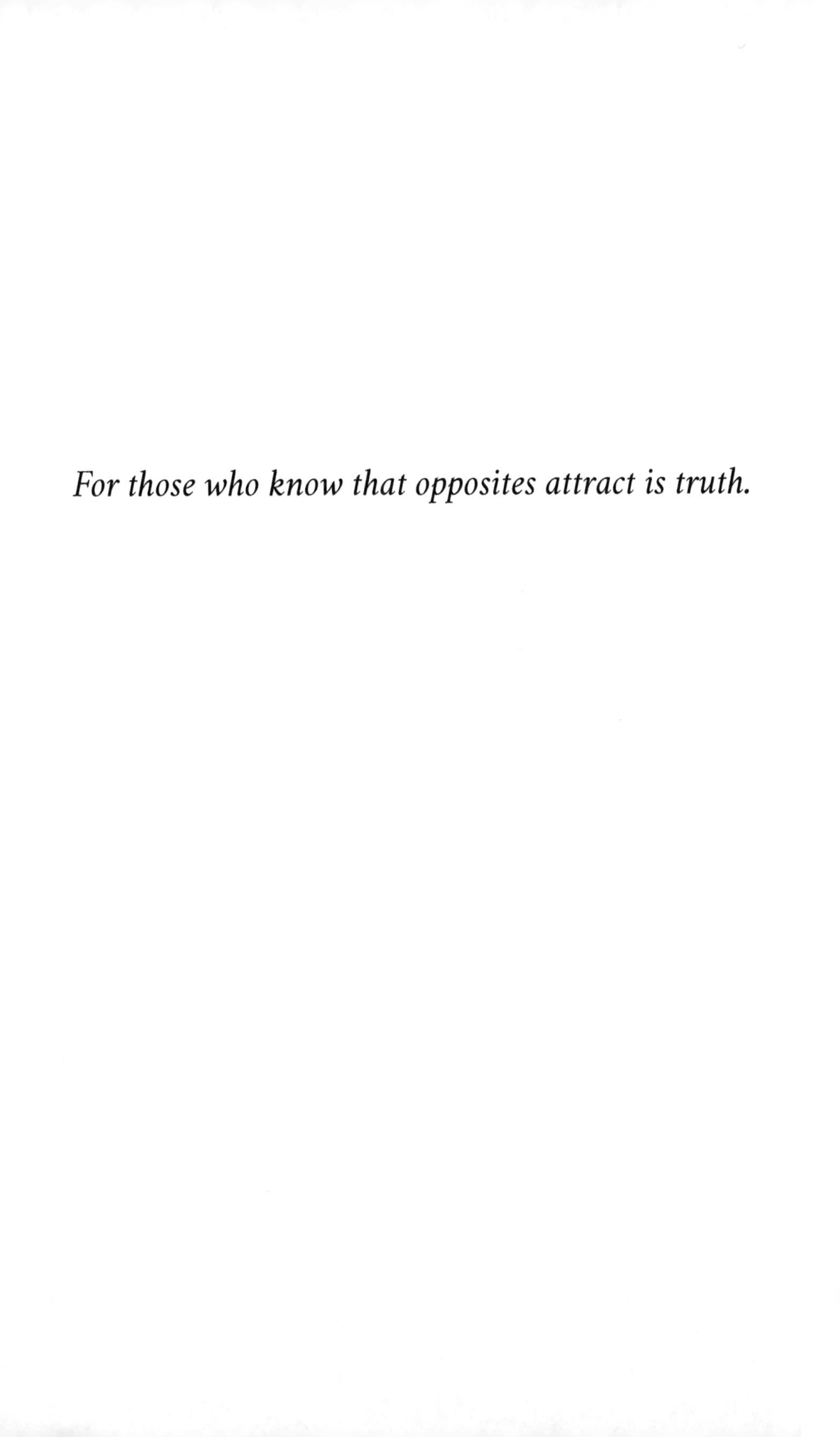

For those who know that opposites attract is truth.

A LETTER TO READERS

Dear Reader,

A few points of note:

A shorter version of this story was originally published as *Once Upon A Wedding*, part of my Meet Cute Romance series. I have expanded it by more than 50% and turned it into a full novella. As such, the original version has been removed from sale.

This book is set in the Deep South. As such, it contains a great deal of colorful, colloquial, and occasionally grammatically incorrect language. This is a deliberate choice on my part as an author to most accurately represent the region where I have lived my entire life. This book also contains swearing and pre-marital sex between the lead couple, as those things are part of the realistic lives of characters of this generation, and of many of my readers.

If any of these things are not your cup of tea, please consider that you may not be the right audience for this book. There are scores of other books out there that are written with you in mind. In fact, I've got a list of some of my favorite authors who write on the sweeter side on my website at https://kaitnolan.com/on-the-sweeter-side/

If you choose to stick with me, I hope you enjoy!

Happy reading!

Kait

CHAPTER 1

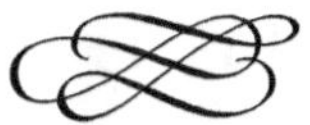

"I can't believe I let you talk me into this insanity." Cayla Black bitched into her white wine spritzer. Denver knew it was the only drink the active, single mom ever ordered, and she was looking at it like she wished it were something stronger.

"Are you backing out?" Kennedy Reynolds' voice held a rare note of panic. His best bartender wasn't prone to panic, and Denver paused in the noisy task of racking glassware before the dinner rush to listen in more closely.

"Oh, I can do it. I didn't say I couldn't do it," Cayla insisted, as though the suggestion that she couldn't mocked her event planner pride. "You just need to be fully aware that your race to the altar is giving me wrinkles. You see this line right here?" She pointed to some nonexistent blemish on her forehead. "I got that convincing Jolene Lowrey to make her prize-winning red velvet cake for your wedding. You're just lucky she has as much fondness for Xander's extremely fine backside as you do."

Kennedy snickered and wiped down the already clean bar. "Your sacrifice is duly noted, but I object to 'race to the altar'. We've been waiting for years. We just didn't know we were waiting."

"Oh, that's…sort of lovely." Cayla's face went soft for a moment, then her brows came back down. "Do not get me sidetracked," she warned, flipping open the bulging planner at her elbow.

Not for the first time since Kennedy had announced her engagement to Xander Kincaid —interim sheriff of Stone County—Denver wondered if there was a bun in the oven. He'd heard the pair had been hot and heavy in high school, but Kennedy had taken off after that, stayed away for a decade, and only resurfaced in Eden's Ridge a few months ago. Xander had just proposed a couple weeks back, and it seemed Kennedy was hell bound and determined to be married next month. What was the hurry, unless there was an oops on the way that they wanted to legitimize before the official election for sheriff in November?

Even as the question crossed his mind, one of his waitresses asked it for him. "Seriously, girl, what's the rush? Did the golden boy knock you up?"

Trish Morgan didn't have a subtle bone in her body and was always all up in everybody's business. But the customers seemed to like her —the men for the T and A and the women for whatever gossip she served up alongside their dinners.

More than used to Trish's less-than-subtle attempts at ferreting out the latest dirt, Kennedy rolled her eyes. "No, we just don't want to waste any more time apart."

"I ought to hate your guts on principle for nabbing one of the Ridge's most eligible bachelors, but it's hard to do that when you look so damned happy."

"Thanks. I think." As Trish sauntered off to finish refilling ketchup bottles, Kennedy turned back to her conversation with her wedding planner. As talk shifted to bridesmaids dresses—oh hell, were those fabric swatches on his bar?—Denver flipped the channel of the nearest flatscreen to ESPN and turned up the volume a bit. Hopefully coverage of the College World Series would help offset the estrogen.

Kennedy did look happy. That hadn't been the case when Denver had hired her a few months back, after her mom's unexpected death in a car accident. Carving out a new niche in Eden's Ridge and within her family had gone a long way toward banishing the shadows from her eyes. But fixing things with Xander seemed to have done the rest. Love conquered all, and all that shit. Denver legitimately liked her—had, right from the start, and he liked seeing her happy. He just hoped her happiness and impending nuptials weren't going to lose him a great bartender.

"—in with Misty Pennebaker."

The name had Denver's attention sharpening like a dog on point. Of course Misty would do the flowers. Even Denver knew she was the only florist in town. He'd taken note of Misty and her flowers every day on his drive to work for the last three years. Hard not to take notice of a woman who looked like she did—sort of neo-hippie flower child, with a smile that could light up Main Street.

But he'd never actually talked to her.

When she'd first showed up in Eden's Ridge, he'd been focused on getting Elvira's solidly in the black, after buying the bar from Len Draper, when the old man had up and decided to retire to Florida. No time for a woman then, and anyway, he hadn't been sure a free spirit like her would stick. But she had stuck, proving that there was more to the pretty brunette than her posies or colorful wardrobe.

And yet he'd done nothing about it.

"Even though it's short notice, she's agreed to meet us here to discuss the options," Cayla was saying.

Denver carefully, methodically stacked the empty trays. Misty was coming here?

She'd been in Elvira's before. Everybody in the Ridge had, at some point or other, for lunch or dinner. But, as a rule, she didn't drink. Since he seldom left his sanctum behind the bar, he'd never had the chance to casually chat her up. Not that he was a casual chat up kind of guy. He could've stopped into her shop on Main Street, but what reason did someone like him have to go in to a place called Moonbeams and Sweet Dreams? There was nobody he wanted to send flowers to or buy a gift for. He had no family. And while he'd made friends in the Ridge, none of them were the kind who'd merit the sort of thoughtful, artsy stuff Misty carried in her shop.

Thanks to the small-town grapevine, he knew she was single, but surprisingly little else was known about her. In a place that valued gossip as highly as gold, that was intriguing all by itself. Since Denver habitually kept to himself too, and he understood valuing privacy, he hadn't tried to find out more. So, he'd just been admiring her from afar all this time, as if she were one of the wild, rare flowers she sold.

Denver hauled the empty plastic trays back into the kitchen, then shoved back through the swinging door to check the syrup levels on the drink fountain. And there she was, framed in the front entrance as the door swung slowly closed behind her. She was wearing one of those bright, flower child dresses that skimmed just below the knees of her very fine legs. The slanting rays of the evening sun teased out traces of red in the dark walnut strands of her hair, spotlighting the trademark crown of flowers she wore. It should have looked ridiculous on a grown woman, but Denver found it unaccountably appealing—a fact which he'd take to his grave and beat anybody for suggesting. She just seemed comfortable in herself, quirks and all. He admired the hell out of that.

"Denver?"

He jolted, realizing from the look on Kennedy's face that she'd been talking to him for more than a second.

"I'm gonna take my break to sort some wedding stuff, okay?"

Ignoring Kennedy's knowing smirk, and the fact that Misty wasn't even looking in his direction at all, he jerked his shoulders. "Yeah, fine," he told her, as he turned to the first patron of the after work crowd. "What can I get you?"

MISTY PENNEBAKER SLIPPED into Elvira's Tavern, pitifully grateful her work day was at an end. Well, there'd be more work with this wedding consult, but that would be fun and for friends. Not that they were friends just yet, but Kennedy bought flowers twice a week for the inn she ran with her sisters, and Misty had hopes they would get there.

She hesitated in the doorway, waiting for her eyes to adjust. She scanned the bar, looking for Cayla and Kennedy, and looked away quickly when she caught Denver Hershal watching her. Even while she avoided it, his gaze had an almost physical weight as it pinned her where she stood. Her skin heated from more than the early June sun, which made no sense at all because he wasn't even smiling. She didn't think she'd ever seen him smile.

The man had presence, and he made her uneasy. Not that she felt threatened by him, despite the tattoos she could see peeking out from beneath his shirtsleeves. He'd never said more than two words to her in the three years she'd been in Eden's Ridge, and she hadn't really done more than nod at him, as was small town custom. Once you were here for a year or so, you knew nearly everyone on some level. But there was something closed about Denver, just one of the things that set him apart from others she had met in the Ridge. He seemed to want to be left alone. Whatever his secrets—and nobody seemed to know what they were, at least not that she'd heard—he had a right to keep them.

Misty saw no reason to push or pry. She understood walling yourself off. Hadn't she done the same? Oh, she'd made friends. She'd made a point of it, as she'd opened her business, gotten to know the various artists and artisans in the area. But there was a very clear line between Now and Life Before The Ridge.

Finally spotting her friends in a booth across the way, Misty broke her temporary paralysis and crossed to join them.

"You are just in time," Cayla crowed. "I've got *ideas!*"

Misty grinned at her enthusiasm. "Kennedy, did you realize you were going to be a guinea pig when you agreed to this?"

Kennedy shrugged. "I needed a wedding planner. Cayla needed someone to practice her event planning skills on to kick off her new business. Seems like win-win to me."

Misty had to agree. A local girl who'd come home to Eden's Ridge after a nasty divorce, Cayla was starting over. Misty knew all about that, and she was all over doing whatever she could to support Cayla's new enterprise.

Over a plate of nachos, they talked budgets and timelines, before finally turning to flower options for the venue—the barn on the family property, behind the inn.

"It's going to be a country wedding, but not redneck," Cayla said. "Tasteful."

"I think Xander was ready to ask me to marry him all over again, when I told him he didn't have to wear a tux."

"You are, without a doubt, the most laid back bride I have ever worked with," Misty said.

Kennedy shrugged, her green eyes dreamy. "I'm just happy to finally be with my Xander."

Propping her chin on one fist, Cayla sighed. "They're disgustingly happy. Join me in my moment of envy."

Misty laughed. "I'm not looking for a man."

"Well, neither am I. I'd like to be more rid of the old one than I am. But damn, I'd love to be that kind of happy."

"Fine," Misty conceded. "Maybe I'd change my mind if I had a guy who looked at me the way Xander looks at Kennedy."

Kennedy squirmed a little. "This is a wedding planning meeting, is it not?"

"Yes, yes, back to work," Cayla said, diving back into her planner and coming out with photos of the barn's interior. "Now, I think we can use some kind of fabric swags or drapes to hide the less attractive sections of the barn, like the hay loft where y'all have stuff stored. And we'll use the crap out of some white twinkle lights and some of that pretty outdoor lighting like you see on restaurant patios sometimes."

"That sounds good," Misty agreed. "And of course, I can use floral arrangements to direct people's attention down the aisle and toward whatever you deem is the front. But it might be nice to have a focal point since there's no real altar. Something to give it some pizzazz."

Kennedy looked intrigued. "Like what?"

"An arbor maybe. Something I can twine with flowers and ribbon. It could be done up really pretty and in your colors."

Cayla clapped her hands once, pressing her

lips together in an obvious effort to hold in a squee.

Misty smiled. "I recognize your lightbulb moment. What are you thinking?"

Instead of answering, Cayla waved her hand. "Denver! Come here a sec."

What the hell? Are we ordering more drinks?

Denver left the sanctity of the bar and strode over, his long legs eating up the distance. "Yeah?"

"How much do you love Kennedy?"

He didn't even blink. "Enough not to complain that her break's run over for wedding planning." It wasn't said in a teasing tone, just matter-of-fact.

But Cayla wasn't put off in the least. "How 'bout enough to build something for the wedding?"

Build something? He's a bartender.

Denver frowned, his brows drawing down over cool gray eyes. "Like what?"

"An arbor. Something Misty can train some

flowers around and on. I've seen your wood-working. It's totally in your wheelhouse." Cayla gestured to the bar. "He carved all that himself."

Collectively, they all shifted to look at the bar, with its subtly beautiful pattern carved into the side panels. Misty hadn't ever really noticed it before because there was usually a crowd of people blocking it. She wanted to get up, get a closer look, but Denver shifted his gaze to her, pinning her in place.

"You want me to build an arbor?"

Something about the way the question was directed at her—or maybe it was just his intense focus—made Misty feel somehow like his target. She pointed at Cayla. "I want someone to build an arbor. She's the one throwing you under the bus."

Cayla clasped her hands in prayer position and gave him The Face—an adult version of the one her four-year-old regularly employed. "*Please,* Denver. For me? For Kennedy? For love?"

He winced. "If I do it, will you stop with all the gushy shit?"

Cayla crossed her heart with one finger.

Face set in lines of resignation, he sighed and looked at the bride to be. "Fine. What exactly do you want?"

Kennedy held up her hands. "Don't look at me. It's Misty's concept."

Cayla shook her head in mock disappointment. "I swear, you'd get married in blue jeans if not for me. Anyway, you are the least fussy bride on Earth. So here's the date we need it by," she scribbled something on a sheet of paper and shoved it across the table at him, "and what we're thinking we can spend on it. Let me know if that doesn't work. You and Misty get together to sort out the details of what she needs and what you can actually put together in that amount of time."

Misty started to protest because Cayla was totally railroading him, but those gray eyes flicked to her again.

"Fine. Dinner crowd's coming in right

now, but I can talk tomorrow. Swing by your shop?"

This big, burly, bull of a man in her pretty little shop? "Uh…okay."

He nodded to himself like something had been decided and walked away, leaving Misty wondering what the hell just happened.

CHAPTER 2

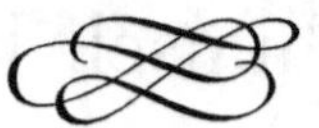

Some kind of bells chimed as Denver tugged open the door of Moonbeams and Sweet Dreams. He glanced up automatically, noting the assortment of wind chimes suspended from a grid attached to the high, tin ceiling—glass, copper, bamboo, wood, other metals. Something for everyone. He shut the door and listened to the quiet tones of drums and flutes that floated out from speakers hidden around the room. Something dreamy and Celtic that suited the tone of the shop. The space was long and narrow, with wide-plank floors he suspected were original to the building. Displays made something of a maze of wares from the front to the back. It reminded him of the lone trip he'd taken to Ikea—herding you through the entire store before you got to the back and the register. Except this was clever, cozy, and warm, rather than a coldly calculated retail corral of gleaming fixtures, filled with a herd of shoppers. Homey instead of Hell on Earth. It helped that there was nobody else here.

Denver wandered through, taking in the pottery, the textiles, the paintings, the carvings, noting the wide and varied selection. Tiny placards explained, in elegant, looping calligraphy, that all were locally sourced from artists and craftsmen of the region. Mixed in with the photographs, the sculptures, the glass, were fresh flowers and plants of all kinds—a seamless blending of the two halves of her business. He could see how somebody might see that vase and immediately want the cluster of whatever those purplish pink flowers were inside it. A girlie somebody anyway, which was her target demographic. As Denver was neither, he found the shortest route to the counter and called out, "Misty?"

Something thumped. He heard a muttered curse and a clatter and wondered what he'd interrupted. She appeared from the back. It was a different kind of flowers in her hair today—something cheerful and yellow, woven into the two small braids pulled back from her face. He caught himself starting to smile at that before he realized she held her hand aloft, blood dripping down her arm.

He didn't stop to think. He just vaulted the counter and snatched her hand. "What the hell happened?"

Misty tipped her head back to look up at him, stammering, "I cut myself on some thorns, while stripping some roses. It's an occupational hazard."

Her hand felt so tiny in his, but it wasn't soft as he'd expected. She worked with her hands, and it showed in the tiny scars from previous nicks and cuts. He lifted his gaze from her hand to her face, catching those brown eyes that were dreamy more often than not. They weren't dreamy now. They'd gone wide and very, very aware.

Denver realized he still held her hand and was all up in her personal space. "Sorry," he muttered, releasing her and taking a step back.

"I…uh…I'm just gonna go wash this and get some antibiotic ointment."

He had the distinct impression she was retreating as she headed back through the curtained doorway into what he presumed was a storeroom and work space. Feeling more than a little bit bull in a china shop, Denver shoved his hands into his pockets and stayed where he was. That's when he noticed the old dog curled up on a bed in the corner. It was a little thing, a ball of black fur, with pointed ears that trembled as she snored quietly. A Pomeranian mix, maybe. Gray around the muzzle.

"Who's your friend?" he called.

"That's Moxie. She was a rescue."

At the sound of her name, the dog cracked open an eye and peered up at him. Denver hunkered down and offered the back of his hand. Looking imperious, Moxie stretched forward just a bit and sniffed. Her little black nose twitched, then she rose and stretched, worming her way under his hand with a sharp little yap that clearly said, "Pet me, damn it!"

Misty came back out, her hand sporting a couple of fresh band-aids. "I got her when I moved to Eden's Ridge because I was finally somewhere I could have a dog."

Following orders, Denver stroked along her little spine, giving the old girl a good rub-down. "Didn't want a puppy?"

"Oh, I love puppies. But seniors need homes too, and I thought it would be easier to keep an older dog with me all the time. Less rambunctious."

It took a special kind of person to choose an older dog, the ones who were usually neglected and first up on the chopping block at overcrowded shelters. He admired the hell out of that.

"Seems like she makes up for that with sass," he observed.

"Hence Moxie," Misty agreed. "Do you have a dog?"

"Yep. Big old mutt. What my dad used to call a Heinz 57 dog. His name's Oscar."

"As in Meyer or The Grouch?"

Denver straightened. "The latter. Though it was because I found him in a dumpster as a pup, not because he's grumpy."

Misty's face twisted with sympathy. "Poor baby."

"He came out all right. And he's sure as hell not a baby anymore. He's a ninety-pound bed hog."

Misty grinned at that and his brain emptied of everything but *Wow.* She had a helluva smile.

They lapsed into silence, Misty watching him expectantly. For his part, Denver was trying to remember what the hell he was doing here. Oh yeah.

"So, about this arbor," he began.

"You really don't have to do this. I can come up with something on my own. Cayla can be a steamroller, at times."

A steamroller who'd given him the in he hadn't managed to come up with on his own. "I'm in it now. Plus, she'll owe me one. Why don't you tell me what you were thinking?" He listened as she described what she had in mind. Spying a sketchpad on the counter, he nodded toward it. "You mind?"

Misty nudged it toward him.

In swift strokes, he sketched out what he imagined, based on her description, thinking he knew just where to get the wood. "Something like this, maybe."

Misty took the pencil from him and began to add to the sketch, refining some details in the carving.

"Are those their initials?" he asked.

"Yeah. Intertwined in a sort of Celtic knot, symbolizing the whole unity of marriage. Can you do that?"

Angling his head, he studied it, seeing how it would work. "Sure."

She continued, drawing out the flowers she'd add. Denver had to admit the overall effect was beautiful.

"Kennedy will love it," Misty declared.

"Well, all right then." Their business was officially concluded. But he was here, in her shop, actually talking to her, and he didn't really want to stop. "We should probably check out the barn, talk measurements and stuff. I expect that would make a difference to how many flowers you'd need, how big I should make the thing."

"You make a good point. I close at five-thirty most days, and I'm closed all day on

Sunday and Monday."

"How about Sunday afternoon? Say, four o'clock?"

"That works for me."

Denver fought back the automatic, *It's a date.* He didn't quite manage to cap the grin as he told her, "I'll pick you up." Then he hightailed it out before he made an idiot of himself.

WEAR PANTS.

Wear pants?

Misty stared down at the text from Denver. What the hell was that about? But she did as he'd asked, unearthing some well-loved jeans that seldom saw much use in the summer. And since she'd gone that far, she paired them with some hand-tooled leather cowboy boots that had seen many, many years' love. The sleeveless, cream peasant blouse made her feel more appropriately summery. Why was she even worrying about what she wore? It's not like this was a date. They were looking at a *barn* for heaven's sake. It was a...business arrangement, really.

Except he hadn't looked at her like he was thinking about business. She didn't actually know what he'd been thinking, but those gun-metal gray eyes had seemed to look *into* her—beyond the polite and the surface she'd limited herself to. How could a look be both disconcerting and appealing?

And he'd told her to wear pants.

Misty finally understood why as she stepped outside her shop at four o'clock on Sunday and saw him cruising down Main Street on a motorcycle.

Oh my...

Bon Jovi's "Dead or Alive" started up as a soundtrack in her head as he pulled up to the curb and shut off the engine. Despite the summer weather, he wore a dark brown leather jacket that hugged his bulk and accentuated that incredible shoulder to waist ratio.

There were racing stripes down the sleeves, which seemed to fit with the lines of the motorcycle between his muscular thighs, currently clad in faded jeans. She couldn't see his face for the helmet, but she knew it was Denver—it wasn't the first time she had noticed the bike, or the biker. Behind the visor, she had the sense he was grinning at her.

Roll your tongue back in, girl.

When he tugged off the helmet, her tongue nearly fell back out of her mouth because, holy hell, Denver Hershal's smile was lethal.

"Hi."

"Hi," she managed.

His gaze skimmed her from head to toe and nodded in approval. "You wore boots, too. Good." He swung his leg over and dismounted —is that what it was called getting off a steel horse like this?

Misty had never really had an interest in motorcycles, but with this bike, and, more likely, Denver and his leather standing in front of it...that could change. "That doesn't look like any motorcycle I've ever seen. It's way more—" She searched for the right word, and almost said "more" again. "—classy looking."

"That's probably because you're used to seeing nothing but Harleys and crotch rockets." Denver ran one big hand lovingly over the dark green tank. "This here is Roxanne. She's a 1981 BMW R100RT, one of the greatest of the airheads."

Misty had no idea what that meant. "Most women wouldn't appreciate being called an airhead."

That deadly grin flashed again, and she felt her internal temperature rise a few more degrees. "It means the engine is air-cooled as opposed to oil- or liquid-cooled, like more modern vehicles."

Misty made a face like that meant something to her, then gave up. "It's pretty," she offered.

He laughed. Serious, monosyllabic Denver Hershal actually laughed. "Yes, yes she is. My dad and I rebuilt her together back when I was in high school." It was obviously a good memory for him. "She's perfect for a Sunday afternoon ride and the weather's beautiful. You game?"

She eyed the seat, which didn't seem to leave a lot of room at the back end. "Is there room for two people?"

"Sure. Gotta get you suited up first, though." He stripped off his jacket and held it for her to put on.

Wait, did she really want to do this?

"What about you?" His t-shirt would hardly provide good protection in the event of a crash.

"We're not going far or fast. I'll be fine." He waited until she'd slipped her arms into the jacket—the sleeves came down past her wrists—and zipped her in. It smelled of leather and man. Misty was still absorbing that, when he unstrapped a second helmet from the back of the seat. He eyed the baby roses in her hair. "Sorry about the flowers. They're gonna get squished."

"Guess it's a good thing I own a florist shop." She reached out for the helmet and slipped it on.

Denver crouched down, shifting, tugging, and adjusting straps, until he was satisfied the helmet fit properly. "All right. You ready?"

Her nerves jumped. "Is that a rhetorical question?"

"Ever been on a motorcycle before?"

"No." She shook her head for emphasis and felt like a bobblehead doll from the extra weight.

"You have the easy job. Hang on to me, lean when I lean. That's it. Easy as pie."

"Pie," she repeated. "Right."

"I'll get on first, then you swing on behind me." He put his own helmet back on, kicked up the stand, and swung one long leg over the back.

There *really* didn't look like enough room on that seat for two people. As if sensing her reluctance, Denver scooted forward a bit.

Pie, she thought again, and swung her own

leg over, using his shoulder for balance. She was right. There really wasn't a lot of room on the seat. Left with the choice of leaving her butt hanging precariously off the back or snuggling up against Denver's back, she chose the snuggle, scooting forward until the insides of her thighs bracketed his ass. It was a very fine ass.

Oh boy.

"You're gonna want to hold on," he said, his voice muffled by the helmet.

Misty closed the face shield and lightly gripped his waist. He cranked the bike and smoothly pulled away from the curb. This wasn't so bad. Nice and easy, as he'd said. Then he shifted gears with a little jerk that had her clenching her hands tighter. When he leaned into the turn off Main Street, and onto the country road that would take them out to The Misfit Inn, she yelped and banded her arms around his waist, plastering herself to his back.

"Relax!" he shouted, laying a hand over

hers, where she was probably squeezing the life out of him.

She forced her muscles to ease a fraction. As the bike gained speed, she tried to focus on something other than the terrifying sensation of not being surrounded by *anything.* What she focused on was him and the curious intimacy of riding behind him. Pressed close, she felt every shift of his body, every flex of his muscle. He didn't have any of her tension. He was a man in complete control.

And Misty liked it.

She also liked the defined ridges of abs she felt beneath her palm. This man was in shockingly good shape for a guy who worked in a bar, and she wasn't ashamed to admit, she wouldn't mind getting to know the rest of him a little better. She wondered if this had been his plan.

The ride was over too soon.

A handful of cars were in the gravel lot behind the inn. Denver bypassed them and pulled right on up to the barn, to a patch of pavement. At his signal, she slid off, using his shoulder for balance again and feeling a little rubber-legged as she stood on her own. He swung his leg off the bike and put down the kickstand before tugging his helmet off.

She did the same. "That was amazing."

There went the grin again. "I thought you might like it. There's nothing like feeling the buffet of the wind and the freedom of the open road."

The feel of the wind. Yeah. Let's go with that instead of the feel of your abs.

Feeling her cheeks heat, Misty looked back toward the house. "Do you think we should go let them know we're here?"

"I talked to Kennedy at work. She already knows we're coming. Said to do whatever we needed to do."

Of course he had.

Misty took off the jacket and laid it over the seat. They hung the helmets on the mirrors and strode inside. He turned all business, pulling a tape measure out from somewhere and getting her to hold the other end as he measured the space, tapping the details into his phone. They discussed placement and height, even lighting. And all the while, Misty watched the easy flex of those shoulders in his t-shirt and remembered the look of him as he'd vaulted over her counter like it was nothing. When was the last time she'd been this *aware* of a man?

The sensation didn't abate as they rode back to town. She enjoyed the return trip more, feeling confident that they weren't going to end up as smears on the pavement. And she saw what he meant about the feel of the wind and the open road, though his body served as an effective windshield for her. She toyed with a question in her mind. By the time they pulled back up in front of her shop, she'd made a decision.

She wanted to know more.

Dismounting with more grace than she'd managed the first time, she pulled off the helmet and shook out her hair like she'd seen in the movies. When the baby roses, now crushed, rained down like some kind of floral dandruff, she figured that had ruined the effect. But it didn't curb her intent.

"Thanks for the ride. It was a lot of fun."

He sat astride his steel horse—Bon Jovi, eat your heart out—and rested his forearms across the handlebars. "Glad you enjoyed it. I'll be getting started on the arbor tomorrow."

Can I come see your workshop? Would he think that was a euphemism? She really did want to see his workspace and how he brought his vision to life. She'd toured more than a dozen different spaces of the artisans whose work she carried. Customers loved hearing little details about how a piece had been created. But this wasn't about her shop. She really just wanted to get to know more about him. So she took a different tack.

"Would you like to come to dinner?"

"I like food," he said equably.

Misty's lips twitched. "Then how about

you tell me what night works for you, and I'll introduce you to some of mine."

"Pick any night."

"What about your shift at the Tavern?"

A flash of humor lit his eyes. "I've got an in with the boss. You let me know when and where, and I'll be there."

She did a quick mental review of her calendar. The early part of the week was slammed, but by midweek she'd be done with the flowers for the monthly Pilot Club ladies' luncheon. "Wednesday? Say seven?" That would give her time to get home after closing, do some last-minute cleaning, and get whatever she was cooking going.

"Sounds good."

Misty gave him her address. "You should bring Oscar. I've got a fenced yard. There's room for him to romp with Moxie."

One brow quirked up. "Does Moxie have enough energy to romp?"

"You'd be surprised."

Denver nodded. "All right, then. Oscar and I will see y'all on Wednesday."

Misty lifted her hand in a wave and waited until he'd cranked the engine again before saying, "Can't wait."

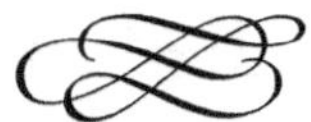

CHAPTER 3

"Pretend you have manners, okay? We're trying to impress these ladies."

Oscar plopped his butt down on Misty's front stoop and, tongue lolling, tipped his head back to look at Denver, as if to say, *See, I got this.* One ear flopped over his eye, making him look a lot more like trouble than a canine gentleman. With a little prayer that the mutt remembered his training, Denver held out the gift bag. Oscar clamped the handle between his teeth and turned back to the door, his baseball bat of a tail wagging so hard, it swept the front stoop.

Man, he hoped this wasn't a mistake. He'd wanted to make a good impression. His grandmama had hailed from Georgia, and, during the formative years she'd helped his father raise him, she'd impressed upon Denver proper company etiquette. It wasn't something he'd been called on much to use in his line of work, certainly wasn't something he or Dad had worried about after her passing. But Denver had heard her voice in his head, telling him he'd best not show up to a woman's house for dinner empty-handed. He'd wrestled over that. What the hell did you bring a florist? Surely not flowers. And that felt too date-like. For all he knew he'd misread things and this was meant to be a playdate for the dogs. So he'd taken a different tack and hoped it was the right one. Gripping the other hostess gift in his hand, and feeling like an idiot, Denver rang the bell.

Misty answered the door a few moments

later, barefoot, with Moxie tucked under one arm and her hair flowing loose around her shoulders.

He said the first thing that sprang to mind. "No flowers?"

"Huh?"

"In your hair."

"Oh, no." She raked a hand through it. "I do that as my own form of free advertisement. Since I'm done with work for the day…"

He wondered what today's flowers had been, but didn't ask. Instead, he held out the tiny parcel in his hand. "This is for the lady of the house."

Seeming a little flustered, she took it. "Oh, you didn't have to do that."

Denver nodded to Moxie. "Pretty sure the queen there will disagree and anyway, Oscar brought yours. Oscar, say hello."

Oscar angled his head and lifted a paw to shake.

"Well, aren't you the cutest?" Misty bent and shook, then accepted the bag. "Ooo, wine.

Thank you, Oscar. This will go great with dinner."

Bullet dodged.

His dog gave a joyful bark and offered up what couldn't be termed as anything other than a broad, flirtatious, canine smile. She grinned back before lifting her gaze to Denver. "Come on through. We'll let the dogs out back to get to know each other, and I'll see what you've brought us."

Denver stepped inside. Her little house was just as fun and funky as her shop, with a heavy emphasis on comfort. Her living room had the kind of furniture you could sink into, with lots of girlie pillows and soft fabrics.

Misty led them through to the kitchen. "I figured you'd be more of a beer drinker."

"You're into carrying the work of local artisans in your shop. I'm into doing the same with local beers, ciders, and wine in my bar."

She paused, one hand on the back door, confirming his assessment that she hadn't known he was the owner. She chuckled. "An in with the boss indeed."

They stepped outside. Her patio reminded him of some kind of foreign bazaar—lots of patterned fabrics draped to make a canopy for shade and an explosion of lush plants made him feel like anywhere but East Tennessee. A couple of rattan chairs were angled to look out over the yard and the view of the mountains beyond. Wine bottle torches were scattered around the perimeter, already lit and giving off the sharp scent of citronella. Off to one side, a huge gas grill was heating.

"That right there is a manly grill."

Misty threw an arch look over her shoulder. "That right there is a fine piece of cooking equipment that knows no gender. Seems I'm not the only one who made assumptions."

"Touché."

Once Misty hit the grass, she set Moxie down. Denver unclipped Oscar's leash. The big dog immediately turned three circles, sneezing all the while, before dropping into a play bow, trembling with excitement. Moxie turned her back on him, then looked over her shoulder with an expression that nearly matched her mistress. With one sharp bark, she took off like a rocket. In a flurry of paws, Oscar raced after her.

"They'll be fine out here. C'mon."

Denver followed her back into the kitchen and accepted the corkscrew she offered.

"I bow to your superior skills in this department, as I value not having to fish cork out of my wine."

He did his duty, uncorking the sauvignon blanc he'd picked up from Temptation Vineyards, while she got out glasses. His buddy, Ford, had assured him it was a great summer choice, no matter what she was serving. "What are we having?"

"Pork kebabs with summer vegetables and fresh chimichurri. And strawberry rhubarb pie for dessert."

"Sounds like it's a good thing I brought my appetite."

She opened the box with the gift he'd brought for Moxie and gave a delighted laugh as she extracted the stuffed crown squeaker toy. "Oh, this is so perfect for her."

"Oscar would kill something like that inside three minutes, but I thought, being tiny, Moxie might make it last a bit longer."

"She's gonna love it." Misty snagged the glass of wine he'd poured her and sniffed. "And I'm gonna love this. Thank you."

"I wasn't sure if you would. You generally don't drink when you come into the tavern."

She went brows up. "Been watching me, Denver?"

Of course he had. How could he not? But saying so could tread perilously close to sounding creepy, and he still wasn't sure where they stood. "Occupational hazard and a small town. I tend to know who drinks, who doesn't, and what they prefer."

She angled her head in acknowledgment. "Makes sense. I know the same thing about people and flowers. To answer the question you're very politely not asking, I never drink if I'm going to be driving. So, unless I'm home or out with my girlfriends and one of them is driving, I don't indulge."

"Sensible."

They carried the wine outside, and once she'd put the kebabs on the grill, they settled into the chairs with their wine.

Misty curled her feet beneath her skirt. "So where exactly are you from, Denver? Not here. There's not a trace of southern to that accent."

"Lake Tahoe. Though I had a grandmother from Georgia."

"You're a long, long way from home."

He sipped at his wine. "It hasn't been home for a number of years."

"So how'd you end up here?"

Being a bartender, Denver was used to hearing other people's stories, not sharing his own. He didn't like revealing much of himself. But he could give her a piece without getting into the whole sorry mess. "From the time I was a little kid, my dad and I planned to take a big ass road trip around the country. We mapped the entire route, all the best motorcycle roads."

"Sounds like fun."

"It would've been." Denver's throat went thick, so he drank more wine. "He died before we could take it."

Sympathy flashed across her face. "I'm so sorry."

A waste. The whole fucking thing had been such a waste, with his dad a victim of all the bureaucratic red tape of insurance that cared more about the bottom line than the people it was meant to serve. Just thinking about it had his hands wanting to curl into fists to pound something. But he wasn't going to get into that whole nightmare with Misty.

Twitching his shoulders, he tried to shrug off the haze of grief and old anger. "After he was—after, I set out on my own. Roxanne got a flat just outside town here, and I had to order a new tire. Picked up a few shifts at the tavern, while I was waiting. I liked the look of the place—the bar and the town—so I stayed."

"Simple as that?"

"Is your story more complicated?"

Something flickered over her face as she considered the question. "Not so much. I finally left a shitty job, and I wanted a real change. A friend of mine gave me a gift—this blown glass globe—I have it hanging in the living room, actually—a gorgeous piece. It seemed like there was a different world contained in this thin shell of glass, colors and shapes, maybe like a better world, waiting to be born." A light laugh and a wave of her hand wiped away the dreamy look that had settled on her face. "The piece always fascinated me, so I tracked down the artist—Hale Copeland, maybe you know him—here in Eden's Ridge. I came. I saw. I decided to stay and open my shop. It was about as far from where I was before as I could get."

"And where was said shitty job?"

"Kansas City." That cloud of…something…

flickered in her eyes again. "I like to keep my distance from that time and place."

"Fair enough." God knew, Denver understood that sentiment. He sipped his wine and met her gaze. "I'm more interested in the now anyway."

The moment caught and held, drawing out until neither of them could mistake his meaning. Then she smiled into her glass. "Now's looking pretty good to me, too."

Two weeks, three lunches, a breakfast, two dinners/playdates for Moxie and Oscar, and a handful of random stop-ins on both sides were more than enough to link Misty's name with Denver's in the local gossip pool. Just that morning, Essie Vaughn, sniffer outer of all brewing romances in Eden's Ridge, had been in Moonbeams and Sweet Dreams asking for confirmation that they were dating. Misty hadn't known what to say because

Denver hadn't made a single move. She knew she hadn't misinterpreted things that first night at dinner. The man was interested. But he hadn't acted on it, and she couldn't figure out why. This was not a friend thing they had going on here. Well, they were becoming friends, certainly. She now knew he'd played in a rock band in college, that he was a closet *Star Trek* fan, and that he had as big a sweet tooth for chocolate as she did. But that wasn't the only thing between them. So what was the holdup?

At least she'd finally wrangled an invitation to see his workshop. They'd finished dinner—pizza from the tavern—and after a romp in the backyard, Oscar had curled up on his dog bed, with Moxie curled up on his outstretched front legs. They were sound asleep.

"I think we have a bit of a May-December romance going on here," Misty observed.

"A what now?"

"A romance where there's a big age gap between the couple. Oscar and Moxie are smitten."

He kicked back against the counter and looked over at the dogs. "I figure he appreciates the value of a woman who knows her own mind." Something glimmered in those gray eyes as he turned back to her.

Were they still talking about the dog? "Moxie can never be accused of being indecisive." Misty passed him the last plate to load into the dishwasher. "So, the furkids are konked out. Are you finally going to let me into the inner sanctum so I can see your progress on the arbor?"

"It's not put together yet."

"I didn't figure it would be. But I'd love to see what you've done so far. Unless you're one of those stubborn artists who doesn't want anybody to see anything but the final product."

"I'm not an artist. Just a guy who likes making stuff out of wood." Denver shoved away from the counter and headed down the short hall. "I ended up making a few changes. It's a lot of work, so I figured I might as well make something they could use beyond just the wedding." He opened a door into what she presumed was the garage and flipped a light.

Misty followed him into the room. Long work benches lined three of the walls, and the air was scented with sawdust and a faint odor of old varnish. Sawhorses with 4x4 posts took up much of the floor space in front of the closed garage door. Various and sundry other pieces were stacked neatly or in different stages of carving. She could see the knotwork design drawn out in pencil on some. She ran her fingers over the pattern already carved in one arched piece. "Denver, I'm gonna argue with you. You *are* an artist. This is gorgeous." *So are you.* She watched his muscles flex as he easily picked up one of the 4x4s, taller than he was, and showed her the design he'd put in.

"I decided it would work best as a small pergola. They can set it up over a bench and create a little seating area or something. The interior crosspieces will be plain, since they mostly won't be seen. But these, the struts, and the lintel that will face the audience will all have this pattern of knotwork and vines. And there will be plenty of space for you to train actual vines or attach whatever other flowers you decide on."

"Where did you learn how to do this?"

"My dad taught me. He was a cabinetmaker by trade. Mostly plain and simple stuff, but every now and again, he'd get a client who'd want something really special. Then he got to play."

"You two were really close." That much was obvious in the warmth of his tone.

"Yeah. It was just us for a long time. My mom split when I was little, and he raised me on his own, with his mom's help. My Nana Jean was from Georgia, but she came all the way out to Nevada and lived with us until she died."

"Sounds like a good grandmother. How old were you when she died?"

"Senior in high school. Wasn't the same after she was gone, but Dad and I managed."

It was the implied tone of *until* that had her pressing for more. "How did he die?" she asked softly.

Denver leaned absently against the post. "He had kidney disease." She thought he was going to stop there, but he kept going. "At first it didn't slow him down much. He kept working, kept training me. Dialysis was just another part of the routine. Then he started getting weaker, having dizzy spells, pain. The dialysis wasn't cutting it anymore. He needed a new kidney. I wasn't a match, so he got on the transplant list. But that's a bit like hoping to win the lottery. He ran out of time."

Misty's throat went thick. The story was so familiar, it made her ache in ways he couldn't understand. "I'm so sorry."

Denver twitched his shoulders. "It sucked. After he died, I couldn't stay. So I sold everything we had left, except for Roxanne and his carving tools, and I hit the road for that trip we'd planned."

Feeling the need to steer them away from this conversational precipice, Misty offered up a smile. "I'm glad you ended up here."

"Me, too." She wasn't imagining the warmth in those gray eyes as they settled on her.

"Answer me this, though. If you can do all this—" She gestured at the workshop and the pieces of the arbor. "—why the bar? Why not make a career out of woodworking or carving?"

"Don't get me wrong, I like building things. Using those tools, designing stuff, that all makes me feel closer to my dad. But doing it as a career, I wouldn't get the choice to do what I wanted, when I wanted. I'd get boxed in to those simple, humdrum designs, and that's not the part I love. Keeping it like this means it stays fun and never becomes work."

"I get that. And I respect it. But there's still a part of me—the part that showcases artisans and craftsmen—that feels like it's a damned shame."

Misty traced the pattern again, admiring the design and the hands that had created it as he put the post back in place. She just generally admired the man himself. His gaze came back to her before dropping to where her fingers were still stroking over the smoothness of the wood. Those gray eyes darkened, and she made her decision. She'd made the first move by inviting him to dinner. That had worked out fine. It was time to up the ante again.

She walked toward him, trailing her hands over the neatly stacked pieces, around the edges of the tools he so prized. "You seem to be a very thorough guy."

One brow arched up. "No point in doing a thing if it's not done properly and well. Take your time and get it right the first time."

"I couldn't agree more." She rose to her toes and laid her lips over his.

For an endless second, she wondered if

she'd made a mistake. Her heart began to hammer with the first tinges of mortification, as he stood, still as the proverbial statue. Then a growl rumbled from his chest. His hands gripped her hips and dragged her against that big, strong body. He might have needed a nudge off the starting line, but he wasted no time in devouring her mouth. And, yeah, he was every bit as thorough as she'd expected him to be.

She didn't know which of them broke the kiss. They were both breathing hard. Her arms were clamped around his shoulders, and she felt positively boneless. As first kisses went, that had been off the charts. She blew out a shaky breath. "I'd call that a properly executed first attempt."

One corner of his mouth quirked. "I don't know, I might need more data to make that call."

Misty grinned at him. "Oh, well, if it's all for science," she agreed, and lifted her lips back to his.

CHAPTER 4

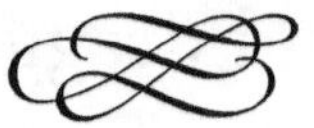

"Well, I guess the lunch rush is over." Norm Barber, the short-order cook at Elvira's, perched one bony hip on a stool in the corner of the tavern kitchen.

Denver eyed the half-load of dishes stacked in the commercial dishwasher. "Wasn't much of a rush."

"Ain't nobody wants to get out in this slop." The older man wiped down the stainless steel counters in reach of his seat. "This rain doesn't stop soon, we'll all be keepin' our eyes out for animals marching two-by-two."

Indeed, the summer thunderstorm had apparently decided to camp out over this chunk of the mountains all day. Denver hoped it would blow out before time to prep for the dinner service. Oscar would go stir crazy without having a chance for a walk or a game of fetch.

"Doubt it'll come to that. But why don't you go on and knock off early? Nobody's coming in this last half hour before the kitchen closes."

Norm slid off the stool, already tugging at the tie of his apron. "Won't say no to that. I heard they're setting up for bingo down at the VFW, and I'm feelin' lucky."

Denver smirked. "With the numbers or with Widow Murchison?" It was hardly a secret that Norm had his eye on Estelle Murchison. According to the local gossip—AKA Trish—Estelle had been looking right back. A first since the passing of her husband a year and a half ago.

Norm's teeth flashed white in his dark face as he slipped on his signature pork pie hat. "Could be with both, if I play my cards right."

Denver laughed. "You old dog."

"Don't knock it, youngin'. 'Sides, rumor has it you got a shot at that yourself with that pretty little florist."

Maybe he did, and he'd given it more than a passing thought. But that was nobody's damned business but his and Misty's. He jerked a head toward the exit. "Go on, old man. I'll see you later."

With another unrepentant grin, Norm saluted and slipped out the back door, into the storm.

The dining room was nearly empty when Denver pushed through the swinging doors. Just a quartet of blue hairs lingering over coffee in hopes the weather would clear. Trish could handle them, while he did inventory behind the bar. He'd barely retrieved his clipboard before the exterior door opened, letting in the sound of driving rain and rumbling thunder. A dripping Misty fought with her umbrella in the entryway.

Denver couldn't stop his automatic smile at the sight of her. She'd pulled her hair back in a braid today. The wind had obviously wrought havoc on the original effect, stripping most of the petals off whatever she'd tucked into the length of it. Only a few straggly pink ones lingered. Several tendrils of hair had pulled free to curl around her face, and more than anything in the world, Denver wanted to kiss her right then.

"So there actually *is* something out there that'll turn your habitual frown upside down," Trish observed. He didn't have to look to note the smirk on her face. The tone of her voice dripped with it.

Without even sparing her a glance, Denver lifted the pass-through. "Go refill the condiments or something."

Misty finished wrestling her umbrella

closed and met him halfway. Conscious they were in his place of business and that tongues were already wagging, he resisted the urge to grab her by the hips and haul her against him.

"Well, this is a surprise. I wasn't expecting to see you until tomorrow." Though he'd already been trying to sort whether he could stop by her shop before time to prep for the dinner rush.

Big, brown eyes met his. "Good surprise, I hope."

"Always." And he was surprised to find it was true. He hadn't ever *not* been happy to see her.

Color crept into Misty's cheeks, but she didn't break his gaze and certainly didn't dim her smile. "I come in search of sustenance. I was slammed this morning prepping for a fiftieth anniversary party, and I haven't had a chance to eat. I was hoping I'd scooted in before the kitchen closed for the afternoon."

Of course, this was the day he'd let Norm go early. "We'll rustle up something." He wasn't helpless behind the grill himself. Grabbing Misty's hand, he led her toward the kitchen. "Trish, man the front."

Tongue-in-cheek, Trish just nodded. "You got it, boss."

As he towed her through the swinging door, Misty laughed. "Ooo. Into the inner sanctum."

Almost before the door had shut behind them, Denver spun, giving in to that primitive urge to get his hands and mouth on her. He drank in her gasp of surprise, curling his hands around her hips and yanking her close, even as she rose to her toes and snaked her arms up his chest. He couldn't get enough of the taste of her, the feel of her, of the helpless little whimper she made as he dove deeper. He couldn't get enough of her, period.

And they were in the kitchen of his bar, where they could be walked in on at any moment.

Cursing his own shit timing, he gentled the kiss and set her away from him.

Breathless, she sagged back against a counter. "What was that for?"

"I missed you." It felt strange to admit it. He hadn't let anybody close enough to miss since his dad died.

Misty's kiss-swollen lips curved in a beaming smile that made something in his chest light up. "I have a confession."

With that smile, it couldn't be anything bad. "What's that?"

"I totally packed my lunch. I just...didn't want it. So I came here instead."

The idea of that had him grinning back. "Then let's see what we can do to satisfy your appetite."

In the beat of silence that followed, his gaze fell back to her mouth, and he thought about satisfying his own appetites with her. When he lifted his eyes back to hers, he found an answering flare of unmistakable lust.

Not the time or place. They were both in the middle of their work days. So he squashed his burgeoning arousal and turned toward the cooler to gather ingredients for…something.

"I don't have quite the breadth of menu options that Norm can make, but I can pull together something. What are you in the mood for?"

"Whatever's easy. A BLT?"

Denver ducked into the cooler to grab the bacon and fresh lettuce. "You're easy to please."

"I mean, anything you fix is going to pale in comparison to the dessert I started with."

Those brown eyes were twinkling at him as he pulled his head out of the cooler. Maintaining a serious expression, he intoned, "Life's too short not to have dessert first."

"I couldn't agree more."

His hand fisted around the rasher of bacon. Why exactly were they still in this kitchen? Oh, right. Because they were both responsible business owners. Damn it.

Striving to pull his mind out of the gutter,

he cranked up the grill and started the bacon. "Tell me about your day."

"Well, you'll never believe who was in buying apology flowers this morning." Misty took Norm's abandoned stool and filled him in. The sound of her chattering about customers and flowers and art was a soothing backdrop as he cooked for her. He realized he felt…happy to do something to take care of her. His hands paused halfway through slicing the tomato. He hadn't taken care of anybody since his dad. Hadn't wanted to. After everything they'd been through, he hadn't imagined he'd ever want to take care of anybody ever again. Then again, making a sandwich was hardly in the same league.

Shrugging off the thought, he presented her with the sandwich.

"This looks amazing." Misty bit in and moaned a little.

The sound of it had his dick twitching.

"This bacon is delicious."

Denver subtly adjusted his jeans. "Fresh from Maxwell Organics."

"It shows." She ceased all conversation and demolished the sandwich, then guzzled the ginger ale he'd poured her.

Amused, he crossed his arms. "Want chips or something?"

"No, this will hold me. I mostly just wanted an excuse to see you." She slid off the stool and put her empty plate in the waiting dishwasher.

"You don't need an excuse to see me." He'd like to see a helluva lot more of her—in every sense.

Crossing over, she laid a hand on his chest. "This isn't high school where the worst consequence of blowing off my responsibilities is maybe tanking my history test. We've got businesses to manage. And on that note, I hate to eat and run, but I've got deliveries to make."

"I thought you had a high school kid helping you with that this summer."

"I do, but he's away on family vacation this week, so it's all on me. It's fine. There are only three, and then I'll be blessedly done for the day."

Denver could still hear the drumming rain on the roof. "The weather is really lousy. Can't you put it off until later? Like tomorrow?"

"Nope. Two of them are anniversaries that are today and one is a birthday. They paid for delivery today, so I shall don my life preserver and row my way out as promised."

Denver didn't like it, but he understood her predicament. "You be careful out there. And let me know when you're back, okay? I'll feel better knowing when you and Moxie are settled in."

"I promise." With another smile, she rose to her toes and brushed a quick kiss over his mouth. "Thanks for the sandwich. I'll see you tomorrow."

It didn't feel like soon enough, but he was on deck to bartend tonight. "I'll walk you out."

At the door, Denver watched her with the bright red umbrella as she fought the wind and rain back down the block to her shop. Another massive roll of thunder shook the windows, and he frowned. He really hated the idea of her on the twisty mountain roads in this downpour. That thought made him pause again. Worrying about somebody else wasn't something he'd been doing since his dad died. Looked like Misty was breaking through all kinds of personal walls. Walls he'd erected to protect himself from ever being stripped down to the bone again.

He didn't know quite how he felt about that. She was more than he'd expected in pretty much every way. As he walked back to resume doing inventory, he realized he was still waiting for the "but." Because so much of his life had come with a "but." He didn't know how to trust that things might simply be right, might simply just line up. He'd never been that lucky before.

Maybe there's a first time for everything.

BY THE TIME Misty finished her two, in-town deliveries, she'd given up on her hair, combing out the remains of today's flowers and gathering the curling mess of it into a knot. Her skirt hung wet and limp against her legs, and she couldn't wait to get home and into a hot bath with a cup of steaming tea to chase away the chill. Or maybe wine. It was five o'clock somewhere and she was almost done with work for the day. But first, she had to brave the rising squall and drive ten miles into the county to deliver this last anniversary bouquet to Jolene Lowrey.

Mother Nature was having some kind of a tantrum, lashing wind and rain against the van hard enough to make it rock as Misty took the road out from town and headed over the pass that led to the next valley. She could barely hear the guiding voice of her GPS telling her where to turn, and the wipers couldn't keep up with the deluge pounding down. She slowed to a crawl, leaning forward, as if that would help her see better. The world had narrowed down to a green and gray blur of the countryside. The drive that should have taken no more than fifteen minutes on a good day stretched into a full half hour. Misty's knuckles were white on the wheel as she turned, at last, into the Lowrey's driveway. The trees of their heavily-forested yard provided some shelter from the wind, and for several, long moments, she simply sat, engine idling, in front of the house.

"Get moving, girl. The sooner you finish here, the sooner you can get home to that bath."

Pulling as close to the front steps as she dared, Misty slipped out into the storm. She didn't even bother with an umbrella. She needed both hands to protect the flowers. The wind snatched at her hair as she hustled up the stairs and rang the bell.

Jolene opened the door, eyes going wide.

Misty managed a weak smile. "Special delivery. Happy anniversary."

"Oh my word! You look like a drowned

kitten. Come inside." The older woman stepped back, opening the door wider.

"Oh, no, I couldn't. I just needed to drop this off."

"Nonsense. This weather's not fit to be out in, and you're practically soaked. Come in and dry off. Have a cup of tea and cake."

That got Misty's attention. "Cake?"

"It's my test run of the red velvet cake for Xander and Kennedy's wedding." Jolene took the flowers and headed on down the hall, leaving Misty to shut the door.

Deciding she deserved some cake after that drive and hoping the weather would clear by the time she left, Misty followed her hostess into a big kitchen. Lingering scents of butter, sugar, and chocolate had her mouth watering.

"These are positively stunning." Jolene buried her nose in the blooms. "It's been forty years and my Curt never forgets."

Misty fisted a hand over her heart and sighed. She absolutely adored this part of her job, seeing love that lasted. Her own parents had been married for thirty years, but theirs wasn't exactly a model relationship. They tended to operate as if spite was an Olympic sport, and Misty regularly wondered why they were still together.

As Jolene disappeared into the adjacent laundry room, Misty called, "So what's your secret to marital bliss?"

She came back with a towel, one silver brow arched. "Looking to train Denver right from the get go?"

Misty's mouth fell open, her fingers going lax on the fabric. "I...we..." The grapevine was apparently ringing. She knew that about Eden's Ridge, but until him, she'd managed to stay more or less below the radar. "That is getting way, way ahead of things. We're just enjoying each other's company and taking things slow."

"Honey, when a man looks like that, slow is not what any sane woman wants."

Misty's brain helpfully shot her back to that kiss in the tavern kitchen, which had been anything but slow. It had been a delicious sur-prise that left her needy and rattled and wishing the kitchen door had had a lock. The man was too potent by half, and she wondered how long it would take to work him around to taking her to bed. No, slow was not what she wanted on that account.

Aware Jolene was soaking up her every re-action, Misty made use of the towel and cast around for a new topic of conversation. A miniature, three-tiered cake graced a stand on the butcher block island. Each tier had a dif-ferent kind of piping. "That's the test cake?"

With a smirk that said she recognized the diversionary tactic, Jolene turned toward the counter. "The real thing will be bigger, of course. But I wanted to test out the layers and play with decorating. I'm afraid my piping skills aren't up to the task. This kind of icing simply doesn't make good flowers."

"It looks lovely. But if you're worried about presentation, you could use real flowers and echo the blooms of Kennedy's bouquet."

She put on a kettle for tea. "Real flowers? I hadn't thought of that."

Relieved the woman had taken the conversational bait, Misty settled in for the discussion. "Yeah, I've done several weddings where they used flowers on the cake. It photographs well and is sometimes less stressful than piping. We'd just remove them after pictures, before we slice it."

"I just might take you up on that."

They discussed options over tea and a slice of the cake—which was every bit as moist and delicious as a blue-ribbon cake ought to be. A half hour later, she had Jolene's order for additional flowers for the cake in hand and the rain had let up a bit.

"I'd better dash before the next wave hits. Thanks so much for the tea and cake, Jolene."

"Thank you for the flowers and the company." She walked Misty to the door. "By the way, I never did tell you."

"Tell me what?"

"The secret to our forty years."

"Oh?"

"We never stop appreciating each other." Her lips quirked into a devilish grin. "In and out of bed."

Cheeks heating, Misty managed to keep a straight face. "I'll keep that in mind." With another wave, she hurried to slide into the driver's seat and backed down the driveway.

It certainly wasn't bad advice. How many people got caught up in the everyday and stopped seeing the little things their partner did to make life easier? How many let stress and work interfere with the maintenance of true intimacy? Probably a lot. As she made her way back toward town, Misty decided she could absolutely get behind a philosophy of always being mindfully appreciative and making time to fall into bed.

Something popped and the van jerked hard. Misty screamed, fighting for control as the vehicle went into a spin. She turned into the skid, certain the screech of tires was the last thing she'd ever hear. Then she was still again, facing a whole other direction. Heart pounding, she lowered her head to the wheel.

"I'm okay. I'm okay." She repeated it over and over, until she managed to pry her hands free and open the driver's side door.

Her legs shook as she stepped out to see what the damage was. The back end of her van hung off the road, and the whole thing tipped at an odd angle. The rear driver's side tire was shredded, and the remaining rear wheel was wedged against a fallen log.

"Okay. I know how to change a tire." But even as she circled around for the spare, she realized there was no way she could get the jack under it with the van in this position. Could she move it to straighten it out? Should she? The road was awfully wet, and the boiling clouds just to the west told her more heavy rain was coming. Was it even safe to try to jack it up? Maybe she should call a tow.

Her phone was in the floorboard. Not damaged, thank God. Turning on her flashers, she put a call in to Thompson's Garage.

"Oh sure, we can do it. But Willie's got two other calls ahead of you. It's gonna be a while."

Great. She was already shivering from the wet and wishing she kept some kind of blankets in the back. She didn't have enough gas to leave the motor running for the heat.

"Well then, I guess put me on the list. If I manage to make other arrangements, I'll call and let you know."

"Will do."

She'd already been out longer than she'd expected. Knowing Denver would worry if he didn't hear from her, she called him next.

He answered on the first ring. "All settled at home with Moxie?"

I wish. "Not exactly."

"What's wrong?"

At the immediate snap of tension in his tone, Misty winced. "I'm fine, but I have a bit of a situation."

"What kind of situation?"

"I had a blowout and it's going to be a while before Willie can get to me. Unless there's some other tow service in town I don't know about?"

"I'll be right there. Where are you?" She hated the urgency threaded through his voice.

"You don't have to do that. You've got work. I just called so you wouldn't worry."

"I'll be right there," he repeated, enunciating every word. "Where are you?"

Maybe his dictatorial tone should have rankled. But it didn't. That stubborn insistence made her go all warm and gooey inside. She didn't have to deal with all of this by herself. For the first time in forever, she had someone she could count on. A super sexy someone whose worry lines she'd kiss away later.

Misty gave him her location.

"I'm on my way."

CHAPTER 5

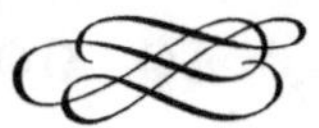

I'm fine, but I have a bit of a situation.

Tension cranked Denver's shoulders tight as he ordered Oscar into the backseat of the truck. He'd come home for a fast game of fetch when the storm died down, but it would have to wait. The dog leapt in, rubber ball clamped between his teeth, as if he sensed now was not the time to dally. It wasn't.

Denver hadn't asked if Misty was injured or what kind of shape the van was in. She'd said she was fine. But his brain readily filled in a multitude of horrors as he drove because he knew better than many that "fine" often wasn't.

I'm fine, but there's something weird on some of my tests. That had been what his dad said. He hadn't been fine. Not even close. Denver knew this wasn't the same thing, but he couldn't seem to stop the churn of anxiety in his gut. The leather on the steering wheel creaked beneath the clench of his fingers. What the hell was wrong with him?

The van sat half on, half off the road, tipped a bit from the flat, but upright and otherwise undamaged. Misty was already sliding out of the driver's seat as he parked along the opposite shoulder. No blood, no bruises, no visible injury, though her cheeks were pale and the hand she lifted in a sheepish wave was a bit shaky. His visual inspection confirmed what his rational mind already knew—she was okay. But he couldn't quite stop himself from pulling her in, running his hands over her.

"You're okay." It wasn't a question anymore. He could see for himself, feel for himself.

Misty reached up to frame his face, forcing him to meet her gaze. "Denver, I'm not hurt. Really. The airbag didn't even go off. The van is fine other than the tire."

Fine. He really hated that word. If she'd blown out two more miles up the road, she might've spun into the rock wall of the pass. Denver rode out a faint shudder. As soon as he got her settled back home and warm, he'd check the other tires and the oil and every other damned thing that could potentially go wrong. When was the last time she'd had it serviced? Who was looking out for her?

But he finally sucked in a proper breath and dropped his brow to hers, feeling himself settle with the contact. He didn't like worrying about her. Didn't like what that said about how important he'd let her become in so short a time. But he liked thinking about all that even less, so he took another breath and stepped back to address the more immediate problem. "We need to get the van moved."

She turned to face it with him. "I wasn't sure if I should move it or if I even could. I mean, obviously it's a road hazard as it is now but the tire is toast. Nobody has been by, thankfully."

Heedless of the rain soaking through his t-shirt and cargo shorts, he circled around the vehicle and immediately saw the problem. The remaining rear tire was wedged against a fallen tree, not in contact with the ground. With the wet roadway, there was no way to get enough traction to pull it straight out.

Denver joined her back at the truck, where she'd cracked the door to reach in and scratch around Oscar's ears. "It's front-wheel drive. I'm gonna hook up a chain to my truck and help you ease it back onto the road and straighten up a bit. Then I'll put on the new tire."

"I really appreciate it." Shutting the door, she stepped into him, eyes searching his face with an expression he couldn't quite read. She squeezed his arm. "Thank you for coming."

Denver laid a hand over hers. "Anytime."

It took longer than he wanted, but eventually they managed to get the van more or less straightened up and out of the flow of the non-existent traffic. He tried to convince Misty to get back inside, out of the rain, but she pointed out that they were both drenched already, so there wasn't much point. Conceding, he hauled out the jack and spare from the back of the van and went to work. Having something physical to do gave him somewhere to put all that nervous energy that had been coiling since she called. The frantic edge was gone by the time he began to tighten the last of the nuts and she'd cancelled the tow from Thompson's.

"You should be all set." Denver replaced the jack and hefted the flat, carrying it over to his truck.

"What are you doing?"

"I'll get this taken care of for you." He set

the rim into the bed of his truck. He'd take a closer look later to see if it needed replacing.

"Oh, you don't have to—"

Denver just leveled her with a look. "I can get away in the middle of the day when they're open easier than you can."

Misty's mouth opened and closed a couple of times, as if she didn't quite know what to do with that. If she thought it violated her female independence or something, that was just too damned bad. He wanted to look out for her, damn it.

"Thank you."

He just nodded. "Go on and get in. I'll follow you home."

She opened her mouth like she was going to say he didn't have to do that either, then apparently thought better of it. "You can at least dry off when we get there."

The rain seemed to have downgraded from thunderstorm to heavy drizzle by the time they got to her little house. He parked behind her van. As soon as the door opened, Oscar scrambled over Denver's lap to race to the van for his own sniff test to verify Misty was okay. Then he spun three quick circles, sneezing the whole time, and bolted for the front door. Denver could hear Moxie barking from inside.

Misty unlocked the door, herding the dogs through the house and out the back. "I'll go grab towels."

Denver didn't stand around. He went straight to the kitchen and started a pot of coffee. She needed to get dry and have a warm beverage. Even as the coffee began to drip, he wondered if she'd rather have tea. He probably should have asked first.

"Oh coffee. Thanks." Misty passed him one of the pile of towels. "Do you have to get back to work soon?"

"It's covered." He'd called in Kennedy to man the bar in exchange for an extra few days off after her upcoming honeymoon. Worth it.

She opened the back door and the dogs streaked in. "Whoa, whoa. Hold up. Paws, Miss Priss."

Moxie barked and delicately lifted one paw at a time for Misty to wipe them off.

Denver lunged for Oscar, managing to get the towel over him before he shook off all over the kitchen. "Manners, remember? Stand still."

Oscar grumbled and fidgeted, twisting to keep an adoring gaze on Moxie, but Denver finally got him as dry as he could. As soon as he let go, the dog rocketed to his lady, barking and sniffing in a play bow. Moxie wriggled, wagging her little tail and prancing off into the living room.

Misty laughed. "Settle, you two. Go take a nap or something."

Her skirt was still dripping on the kitchen floor, her skin pebbled into gooseflesh in the air conditioning. Now that the crisis, such as it was, was past, Denver had a moment to take in the rest of her. The skirt molded to her full hips and perfect ass. The hair plastered in wet tendrils to her cheeks and neck. The cotton tank that clung to her breasts was one of those deals with a built in bra, and it did nothing to hide the nipples pearled from the cold.

A rush of heat shot straight through him as he thought about taking those nipples in his mouth.

Not the time. Curling his fingers into his palms, Denver jerked his eyes back to her face. "You're soaked to the skin. You need to change into dry clothes and warm up." Okay, so his voice had gone rough as sandpaper. He was only human. But he could still be a damned gentleman.

She grabbed one of the other towels and strode over to him, big brown eyes warm and sparkling. In one, quick motion, she looped it over his head and around his neck to tug him closer, until barely an inch separated their wet bodies.

"I definitely agree with getting out of wet clothes, but I have other ideas for how we can warm up."

Now it was his turn to gape like a damned fish. "I wasn't expecting…You don't have to…"

One corner of her mouth kicked up. "This isn't because you rescued me. Although I'm happy to show my appreciation on that front. I've been thinking about this since that kiss in your kitchen. Longer, really."

Well, shit, so had he. He curled his hands around her hips, loving how the lush curve of them fit in his palms. "I figured to romance you a while longer."

"Oh, you can still do that. But I don't see any reason why that should preclude getting naked together."

Whatever blood was left in his brain drained south.

Misty tightened her hold on the towel and rose to her toes, bringing her mouth within a breath of his. "I know you like for things to be crystal clear, so consider this my enthusiastic consent. Take me to bed, Denver."

AT HER WORDS, Denver's eyes went dark as storm clouds. He growled, a deep, primal sound that made all Misty's girly parts flutter in anticipation. Then his mouth was on hers in a claiming kiss. No hesitation, just raw need and enough heat she wondered that the water didn't simply evaporate off them both.

God. This was what lay behind that ruthless control of his. Power and a potent hunger. For her.

Misty thrilled at the idea of it, at the taste of him flooding her mouth as she opened for him. His hands curled around her hips in that possessive way she'd come to love, and she pressed closer, feeling the bulge of his erection straining against the zipper of his cargo shorts. She needed to touch him. To see him.

Releasing the towel, she tunneled her hands under his shirt, breaking the kiss long enough for him to wrench it up and off. The fabric hit the floor with a sodden thud. When he reached for her again, she held up a hand, pressing it to his muscled chest.

"Let me look at you."

He was utterly beautiful. Swirls of ink accented the defined muscles of his chest and arms. Before she could do more than run an admiring hand over him, Oscar brushed against her leg and began nosing at the shirt, opening his mouth. Misty grabbed it before he could snatch it up. "Oh no you don't."

Denver shot an exasperated glance at his dog. "We should probably relocate."

"Definitely." She led him into the laundry room.

He eyed the washing machine. "I mean, not what I was expecting, but the height is good."

Misty snorted. "Not where I was going with that. Practicalities before fun. If we throw your clothes in the dryer now, the dogs can't mess with them, and they'll be ready later."

"Planning to get rid of me so soon?" He shucked his pants and boxers as he spoke and her mouth went dry, even as her body flushed.

Jolene was wrong. Any sane woman would

want to go very, very slow with a man like him. Preferably all afternoon and into the night.

"No. In fact, I might just hide your clothes altogether." She tossed them into the dryer.

He smirked, the expression surprisingly boyish on his usually serious face. "I'm only good with that plan if you're playing, too."

The quicker she got naked, the quicker they could get to the fun part. "I mean, it's only fair." She slipped her fingers into the waistband of her skirt and shoved it over her hips and down.

The molten heat in his eyes as they traced over her was its own pleasure. When she reached for the hem of her tank, he stopped her.

"Let me." He inched it up himself, trailing his work-roughened fingers up her torso, brushing the sides of her breasts, until he stripped it off, leaving her bare, but for a thong.

Misty shivered, but not from the cold.

Swearing, low and reverent, Denver boosted her up until her legs could wrap around his waist. "Which way?"

"Wait!" Leaning over, she swatted at the controls of the dryer until it turned on. "Let's go."

Breathless from the feel of all his skin against hers, she directed him toward her bedroom. Somehow he navigated furniture and dogs, getting them through the house in record time. He kicked the door shut, right in a pair of over-interested canine faces. Their whines of affront sounded through the wood as he tumbled them both onto the bed.

Denver wasted no time in stretching over her and feasting on the hollow of her throat. Humming with pleasure at the glorious weight of him, Misty tipped her head back to give him better access.

Someone scratched at the door.

"Moxie, go lay down," she groaned.

Moxie barked her protest.

"Sorry. She's not used to being shut out."

There'd been nobody to shut her out for since Misty had brought her home.

Oscar barked.

"Hush it!" Denver kissed his way lower, down to the valley between her breasts. "He's got no clue what's going on either. Do we need to actually lock the door?"

"As long as it latched, we should be… mmm…fine."

"Bet I can make you forget they're out there."

"Oh, please do."

He closed his lips around her nipple and sucked.

Misty arched up, spearing her hands into the short, brown strands of his hair to hold him there. "Definitely more of that."

He lavished her breasts with attention from his mouth and those wonderful hands, until she writhed beneath him, needing more. When he finally broke away to move further down her body, hooking his fingers into the waistband of her panties, she almost sobbed in relief.

Then he paused, pressing a stubbled cheek to her belly with an expletive that was far less than reverent.

All but vibrating with need, she met his gaze. "What's wrong?"

"Condom. I don't have one."

Releasing a breath, she relaxed a fraction. "Nightstand. New box. Picked them up on a trip into Johnson City last week."

Denver angled his head. "Really?"

Suddenly self conscious, Misty squirmed. "I mean, I hadn't exactly been expecting to be using them this soon, but I didn't know when I'd get the chance for out-of-town shopping again, and I wasn't keen on fueling additional speculation about us in the gossip mill."

His grin flashed again as he grabbed the box out of the drawer. "God bless a well-prepared woman."

Protection in easy reach, he went back to driving her insane. He was as slow and thorough in bed as he was with everything else. By the time he'd wrung one toe-curling orgasm out of her and driven her up again, Misty was ready to beg.

"Please. Please."

He took his sweet-ass time making his way back up her body, trailing soft, languid kisses on her knee, her thigh, the crest of her hip, before he reached toward the bedside table. Foil ripped. Moments later, he settled over her, into the cradle of her hips. He held there, arms braced on either side of her head, staring down at her for a long moment before he murmured her name and pressed into her, one slow, aching inch at a time. He didn't say a word, just watched her with fierce concentration. Misty could only stare helplessly back, her throat going thick with emotion. There was something else here—a tenderness beneath the heat that made her heart stumble in her chest. She trembled, at the cusp of something so much bigger than simply giving him her body.

Half wondering, half afraid, she reached up to cup his cheek. He turned his head, brushing a kiss to her palm. Then he began to move and she lost the thread of fear in the sounds and sighs of pleasure. Cocooned in the premature gray twilight, as rain continued to drum on the tin roof, he loved her well, drawing out the climb until they both shattered.

Afterward, as their breaths slowed and sweat-slicked skin cooled, Denver held her close. It felt right to be curled up against him, her legs tangled with his. But still, the worry trickled in. When she'd decided to take him to bed, she'd thought it would be easy. An inevitable conclusion to the chemistry sizzling between them. Simple and mutually pleasurable.

But she'd seen his face, felt the way he'd cherished her. She could no more hold back her own response to that than to take back the orgasms he'd given her. What was between them wasn't simple or casual anymore. It was more than she'd expected. He was more than she'd expected.

"You're thinking awfully hard," he rumbled.

"My brain is trying to come back online and failing," she lied.

She didn't dare ask him how he felt. Not yet. She knew him well enough now to understand that fast would never be his way. He wouldn't be ready to face whatever she'd seen in those unguarded moments. Pressing him on the issue would be a good way to ensure a swift retreat. And anyway, she wasn't entirely ready to face the truth herself—that she was more than half in love with him already.

He'd catch up eventually. She had faith. Meanwhile, she tucked the knowledge close to her heart and rolled to straddle him, intent on distracting them both.

CHAPTER 6

"I had a to-go order."

Across the counter, Crystal Blue, proprietress of Crystal's Diner and current pain in Denver's ass, pursed her lips. "I'm not handing over those sandwiches until you confirm or deny the rumors."

"Holding takeout hostage in the name of gossip is a low move, even for you, Crystal."

"What is the big deal, Denver? Everybody knows you and Misty have been spending loads of time together this past month. And don't even try to tell me it's just for the sake of Kennedy and Xander's wedding. I want to hear it straight from the horse's mouth. Are you and Misty Pennebaker together?" She fisted her hands on ample hips and stared him down.

When Denver just stared back, Crystal stamped her foot. "Is she your girlfriend?"

"If I say yes, will you give me my sandwiches, while they're still hot?"

"As long as it's not a lie."

"Then yes." Not that they'd talked about it since he'd stumbled out of her house in the wee hours a couple days ago, but Misty didn't strike him as someone who'd be casually knocking boots without some kind of commitment. They should probably discuss that.

"I *knew it!*" she crowed.

"Then why did you have to harass me about it?" Denver muttered.

"Oh, shut up and take some pie to your sweetheart." Crystal boxed up a slice of cherry and added it to the bag before handing it across the counter.

"How do you know that's where I'm going?"

"Because you ordered the grilled mac and cheese sandwich with curly fries, which is what she always orders."

"So does half the town. It's your best-selling sandwich."

"Yeah, but the rest of the town doesn't make you smile."

Realizing he was grinning like the damned Cheshire Cat, Denver pokered up. Crystal just smirked at him. Time to go.

"Tell Misty I said hi!"

"You wanted to live here," he reminded himself as he hit the sidewalk. But this was the first time he'd been the center of attention since the year he'd moved to the Ridge. He kept to himself, kept off their radar, and he liked it that way. So did Misty. Well, they were in it now. He'd probably best confirm the status of their relationship himself before it got back to her that he'd up and made a public announcement in the diner.

Denver was still pondering how to broach that subject as he opened the door to Moonbeams and Sweet Dreams. He knew instantly that something was off. Pausing just in the threshold, he scanned the shop. Nothing seemed out of place. Then he realized there was no music. Maybe she was picking a new playlist. He headed for the back.

"Misty?"

"In the back." Her voice lacked its usual cheerful enthusiasm.

Oh God. What if something had happened to Moxie? Braced for the worst, Denver quickened his pace. As soon as he rounded the counter, the little dog leapt up from her bed and rushed over, demanding attention. He loosed a breath and scooped her up, giving her an automatic cuddle as he continued into Misty's workroom.

She sat at a table. Beside her was an open wooden crate, spilling packing material onto the floor. On the table itself was an enormous glass…something or other. It was obviously art of some kind, but that was as much as he could tell.

She swiveled on her stool and mustered up a smile. But it was a weak facsimile of her norm. "Hi." She seemed dimmer somehow, not at all herself.

Denver set the food on a shelf. "I brought lunch."

"That was sweet. Thanks."

"What's wrong?"

"Nothing."

"Are you saying that because you don't want to tell me or because you're trying to convince yourself you're not upset about something?"

The pale smile flashed again. "Maybe a little of both."

He set Moxie down and fished out the dog biscuit from his pocket. She snatched it from his grasp and went trotting back to her bed. Hands free, Denver framed Misty's face, brushing a gentle kiss over her lips before combing her hair back with his fingers. "Talk to me."

She turned to look at the glass thing on the table. "It's beautiful, isn't it? Hale's work. He always sends me something truly exquisite on this day."

"Why today?"

"Trying to cheer me up, I suppose." She sighed. "You remember I told you that I ended up here because a friend had given me one of Hale's pieces, and I tracked him down?"

"Yeah."

"Judy wasn't a typical friend. She was this woman I got to know through my job. I was the managed care specialist at her HMO."

A sick feeling set up in Denver's gut as he grabbed another stool and sat across from her.

"She first called in because of a denied claim. It was a common enough thing. The insurance industry is obnoxiously and needlessly complicated."

He knew that from so much first-hand experience. The memory of all those phone calls and emails began to bubble and froth as Misty spoke, and he had to fight to keep his focus on her.

"People were usually pretty upset by the time they got to me. I can't tell you how many times I got told off. But Judy didn't do any of that. She was the sweetest thing. Said she was sure there was some kind of a mistake and that she had faith that I could fix it. I told her I'd do my best and that she might want a snack because this kind of thing of thing took a while. She said she was making cookies, and we got off on this tangent where she told me all about her recipe for snickerdoodles and how they were her grandchildren's favorite. I took down all of her information to look into the situation and promised to call her back. She sent me snickerdoodles the next day."

Even as the memory made her smile, that sick feeling continued to grow in his belly.

"A lot of my job was sorting out the complicated legalese of contracts—I'd gone to law school, if you can imagine that."

Law school? How had he not known this about her? "I have a really hard time seeing you in a courtroom."

"So did I. That's why I dropped out after my second year. But I understood contracts, and I kind of fell into this job. I certainly didn't love it. Didn't even like it most of the time. But I was drowning under my parents' disapproval and massive student debt for a degree I didn't get. Anyway, so I started digging into Judy's case. It took a while. I had lots of cases. Lots of details and minutiae to sort through. Sometimes I'd call her. Sometimes she'd call me. But we ended up talking a few times a week. I'd update her on the great big nothing I was accomplishing, apologize for the system, and then we'd just talk about life stuff. Those calls were the highlights of my week."

"Did you get her sorted out?"

"For that first claim, yeah. But while I was

messing with all that, her condition got worse."

Of course it did. Because that's how it went. That's how these companies worked.

"Her doctor said she needed a particular procedure. So she started all the pre-approval paperwork, but it got hung up. That part wasn't even on me, but I knew the system better than the person assigned to it. She needed that surgery." Misty's voice shook. "I managed to parse out that the problem was a conflict between her primary policy and her Medicare supplement. The procedure her doctor wanted to perform was not the conventional treatment. He'd said the conventional wouldn't work and he wanted to take a more aggressive approach. The way the contracts were written, neither insurer was actually going to cover it without exhausting all the conventional—aka cheaper—options first. Because why on earth should insurance we pay for cover the things we actually need, right? She couldn't afford a three hundred thousand dollar surgery out of pocket."

Denver tasted the bitterness of her tone on his own tongue. Old fury boiled up inside him, making him want to howl.

"I couldn't tell her that. I couldn't tell her that there were no more options. So I put her off, and I researched my ass off, trying to find something, anything that could help her. By that time, we were talking every day. And then one day, she didn't call. And she didn't answer when I called her house."

He knew how this would end before she said it and curled his fists against the futility of it.

"Another day passed, and another. And I finally found it. The damned loophole she needed to get her surgery paid for. When I still couldn't get her by phone, I went to her house. We had her address in the system. I was breaking all sorts of rules, but I had to tell her. It was a young woman who answered the door. A few years older than me. She'd been crying. Somewhere deep down, I knew. But I went ahead and introduced myself and asked if I could speak to Judy." Misty sucked in a breath and blinked back tears. "She'd died two days before."

Denver closed his eyes, fighting back the choking rage. "Too little, too late," he bit out.

"Yeah. I expected her to slam the door in my face. Instead, she invited me inside. She said her mother had talked of me often, and she'd left me something in her will. I couldn't imagine what. We were...well more than strangers by that point, but..." Misty trailed off, struggling against emotion. "She'd left me the globe. It was beautiful. All bleeding colors and this sort of vignette inside that looked like the moon and stars. She said it was called Moonbeams and Sweet Dreams, and it had been one of Judy's favorites. I didn't know then what it was worth, but I thanked her daughter and took it. Then I turned in my letter of resignation. I didn't know what I was going to do next, but there wasn't a chance in hell I could go back to that job. Eventually, I ended up here. I started this shop as a way to honor her memory."

Misty lifted her gaze to his. "Today is the four year anniversary of her death. It always gets me down."

She needed comfort and kindness. Denver recognized that. But he couldn't seem to make himself lift his hand to touch her.

She was one of them. A part of the system that had killed his father and broken his life. An unwilling part, but a part nonetheless. And he couldn't unsee that, couldn't unknow it. He couldn't chain down his anger. Not now.

"I'm sorry." They were, if not the right words, acceptable words. They were all he could manage past the noxious swirl of shit her story had stirred up. He needed to get the hell out of here before he spewed any of it out and made everything worse. She didn't deserve to be the target of his unfettered resentment. "I hope the sandwich helps. I have to go."

"Go?" She blinked, those big, trusting brown eyes he suddenly couldn't look at anymore. "You're not staying to eat with me?"

"No. I have a…thing." Denver took a step back, then another. "I'm sorry," he repeated, and walked away.

"It's open!"

In response to Cayla's shouted invitation, Misty opened the front door and stepped into chaos. The cushions from the sofa were scattered on the floor. A bowl of popcorn was up-ended in front of the TV, where *Frozen* was playing at low volume, and a half-full sippy cup lay abandoned on the coffee table. Even as she watched, a giggling four-year old went streaking down the hall—literally. The kid was naked as the day she was born.

A harried-looking Cayla chased after her. "Madeleine Faith, you get your tush back to the bathroom. It's time for your bath!"

Already up to the middle name. Clearly the night wasn't going well. Now Misty understood why Cayla had asked her to stop by her house instead of bringing the ribbon she'd picked up by the shop.

Shutting the door behind her, Misty dumped her purse and stepped into the hallway. When the little girl came racing toward her, Misty scooped her up and blew raspberries on her belly. "I spy a dirty little girl." Indeed, a fair portion of whatever had been for dinner was smeared all over her face. Mac and cheese had definitely been part of the menu.

"No!" Maddie giggled.

"Don't want a bath?" Misty asked.

"No!" Maddie shouted. "I'm a princess! I don't have to."

"Princesses have to be clean. It's in the handbook."

"What's a handbook?"

Misty began walking down the hall, carrying the squirming bundle of little girl. "It's like the Princess Rulebook. Elsa and Anna are always clean, aren't they?"

Maddie screwed up her face in thought, and Misty prayed she hadn't misremembered the movie.

"Yeah,' Maddie admitted slowly.

"Don't you want to be a princess like Elsa?"

Maddie shrieked a fresh giggle. "I wanna be a reindeer like Sven!"

"But then you'd have to eat hay. You don't wanna do that, do you?"

She made a squished face of disgust. "I don't like hay."

"Then princess it is. And princesses take baths." Misty set her into the tub, which was already filled with bubbles. "And check it. Your mom put in these cool colored bubbles. They're *blue,* just like Elsa's dress!" She scooped up a handful and set them on Maddie's head. "There, now you have a crown."

Maddie preened.

"If you play quietly and finish your bath,

you can have two stories tonight before bed," Cayla promised from the doorway.

"'Kay."

"Mommy and Miss Misty are gonna be right out here, okay?"

But Maddie was already lost in her adventure, which Misty was pretty sure was a reenactment of Elsa and Anna's parents' ship sinking.

Cayla stepped into the hall and blew out a breath. "Thanks for that. It's been a…day. And thank you for coming by. I'm sure I interrupted plans with Denver."

It was Misty's turn to blow out a breath. "You'd be wrong. I haven't spoken to him in a week." Not since he'd so abruptly left her shop.

Cayla frowned. "What? Why? Did y'all break up?"

"Breaking up would imply we were formally together in the first place." Which, yeah, okay, she'd thought they were—or at least had been heading hard in that direction.

"What happened?"

"I have no idea. Things were good. Great, even. Or so I thought. Then last week he came by the shop with lunch from the diner. It was the anniversary of Judy's death, so I was pretty down. He wanted to know what was wrong, so I told him about her. And something about that set him off." Misty had played the whole thing over and over in her mind and couldn't figure out the problem. What had she said? What had she done?

"Was he ugly to you?"

"No. He just hightailed it out of there. Left his own lunch in the process. I've tried to call him all week, but he's not answering or returning my calls. I even went by one day, but he didn't answer the door." Yet a new tire had been waiting for her at the back door to the shop. No note. Maybe that was a message in and of itself.

"Have you been by the tavern?"

"No. I'm not going to confront him in his place of business. And even if I were the kind of woman to do that, Trish Morgan is the biggest gossip in town. We both value our privacy."

Cayla crossed her arms and scowled. "That just doesn't make any sense. That's not how it was supposed to work."

"How what was supposed to work?"

"Oh, Denver has had a thing for you for years. So Kennedy and I conspired to throw you two together so he'd finally get to know you instead of just watching from afar."

She'd wondered what that whole steam roller routine was about. "Yeah, well, obviously reality didn't live up to expectation." It was the fear that had kept her tossing and turning every night since he'd walked away.

"Misty Pennebaker, you stop that right now."

Misty had to smile a little at the mom voice. "Yes ma'am."

"I'm serious. You are awesome. And by all indications, Denver agrees with that assessment. So we need to figure out what's got his panties in a wad."

"*We* don't need to figure out anything but the last-minute details for Kennedy's wedding. Seriously, Cayla, I just want to do this job and go back to my shop." *So I can lick my wounds in private.*

"So you don't want to know what happened?"

Misty threw up her hands. "Of course I do. But what if I don't like the answer? What if he decided he doesn't like forward, pushy women? Because I had to make all the first moves in this relationship. I asked him to dinner. I kissed him first." *I seduced him first.* Maybe sleeping with him had been jumping the gun, but she couldn't figure out why. "I'm not going to make the move to chase after him. That smacks too much of desperation, and I've got some pride left."

Cayla sighed. "Well, I don't like it, but fine. I promise I won't do anything."

"Thank you."

"Even if he does need a crowbar to pry his head out of his ass," she muttered under her breath.

Misty mustered a smile. "Maybe he'll get there on his own. Eventually." But she wasn't holding her breath.

CHAPTER 7

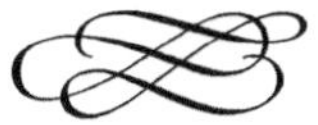

Denver opted to do the final assembly of the arbor on-site at the barn of the inn. That way, he could do everything himself and not have to actually talk to anyone. Talking was the last thing he felt like doing. After six years in this town, keeping his head down and out of the local gossip, he'd managed to put himself right, square in the middle. He'd resorted to glaring his employees into silence and otherwise avoided everyone else by sticking to his tiny office in the back, catching up on the books. He thanked God for the fact that he owned a tavern, otherwise he'd have been forced to actually go to the local market and face the masses or starve. In his current mood, starving was the more appealing option.

He backed his truck up to the barn doors and quietly dropped the tailgate. There were multiple cars in the gravel lot, among them Kennedy's. But he knew her sisters had made it into town, so he was hoping she stayed tied up with them long enough for him to get in and out. His plan held for about half an hour.

"Oh my God, it's gorgeous!"

On the ladder, Denver closed his eyes and repressed a curse. Five more minutes and he would've been gone. Instead of looking at Kennedy, he continued to tighten the nut that held on the elaborately carved front lintel. "Glad you like it."

She circled around and looked at the thing from all sides, and all the ooing and ahing was gratifying to his ego. He'd done a damned good job on this thing. She stayed silent as he attached the cross pieces that lined the top. When he was finished, he climbed down and they both stood taking in the finished product.

"I can't thank you enough. I had no idea you were this talented."

Denver shrugged. "You're welcome. The whole thing has been weather sealed, so after the wedding, if you want, you can use it somewhere in the yard—here or at your place."

She clapped her hands and grinned. "That's brilliant!"

He thought about saying something about how Misty had said they could plant some kind of flowering vines to train up it, but that would be opening the very subject he wanted to avoid, so he just nodded and began to gather up his tools.

"Now that's out of the way," she said, "what the hell's the matter with you?"

His hand tightened on the socket wrench and he chilled his voice down to a glacial tone that had cowed lesser men. "Excuse me?"

Kennedy was no man. "What did you do to Misty?"

"I didn't *do* anything." Well, he'd run like a coward and avoided her for a week. That left a bad taste in his mouth, but he just couldn't deal with what she'd told him. How could he look at her now and not think about the reason his father was dead?

"You hurt her."

Damn it. Was this going to be some kind of girl code ass kicking? Denver turned away, putting his tools back into the box. He knew he'd hurt her, and it made him feel like an asshole. But what could he say to her? Hey, now that I know this thing about you that you can't actually change, you remind me of the worst time of my life, and I can't look at you anymore? No. She deserved better than that, and he hadn't figured out what the hell that was.

Kennedy moved to the opposite side of the truck, right in his line of sight so he couldn't fail to see the pinch of disapproval on her face.

"I saw you two together. Things were good. Y'all were happy. So what changed?"

She wasn't gonna let this go unless he gave her some kind of a reason. "I found out something about her past that I'm having trouble dealing with."

"What? Did she kill somebody?" Sarcasm fairly dripped from her voice, but something must have shown on his face because Kennedy sobered. "Wait, did she?"

"No. No she tried to help." She'd tried to help, but it hadn't been enough.

Kennedy frowned, clearly trying to work through his logic without him spelling it out. "Did she do something in trying to help that directly caused someone to die?"

"No. It wasn't directly in her hands. Not really." Misty had done her job. Gone above and beyond, actually, trying to find some way to get Judy what she'd needed. She hadn't set the rules she'd been bound by, and she'd broken them trying to do the right thing. It was more than anyone had done for his father.

Would things have been different if they'd had someone like her on their side?

"Then it's in the past. Speaking as someone who's spent a lot of her life being driven by the past, it's best to let it go. Unless whatever it is she did fundamentally alters who she is for you. Does it?"

Someone else would have stayed in the job. Someone else wouldn't have acted in the first place. Someone else would simply have said, "Sorry, this is the policy," and left it at that. Denver had dealt with those someone elses. Endlessly. But Misty had quit. And she'd changed her whole life to build something beautiful to honor a woman whose life had touched hers. The whole thing had made her into the woman he so admired. The woman he couldn't stop thinking about.

Arms braced on the side of the truck, he dropped his head. "I know I need to apologize." And if he wasn't such a chicken shit, he'd have done it already. But finding the words to explain wasn't exactly easy. It would rip him open to tell her the whole thing, and he didn't know how long it would take to scab over again. Or if it would heal at all with a fresh reminder every time he saw Misty.

Kennedy nodded. "I have it on good authority she's working late tonight prepping stuff for the wedding."

"What the hell am I going to say?" Denver muttered.

"The truth," she said simply. "Whatever it is, it's better to get it out there. Trust me on this." When he said nothing, she shot him a piteous look. "Don't waste the chance Cayla and I bent over backward to create for you."

Denver met her gaze. "We aren't talking about that."

"Are you going to go talk to her?"

"Yeah." His conscience wasn't going to give him a choice. He didn't know if he actually *could* go back to thinking of her as the clever, intriguing woman who made him feel connected again for the first time in years. But he owed it to her to apologize for blowing her off without an explanation. And he owed her the damned explanation, even if it meant baring things he'd kept buried for years.

"Then we won't talk about how it took two nosy women to get you over your own inertia." She slapped the truck. "Go on. Go fix this."

"Yes ma'am," he said and slipped into the driver's seat.

THE WIRE FRAMES had been a pain in the ass to build, but Misty thought she'd finally managed what she wanted. The pair of them ought to give the structure she needed to hold up the massive sprays she intended to mount to either side of the arbor. She'd be doing most of the rest on-site the night before and the day of the wedding, but having this piece finished was a load off. Her supplier had dropped off the flowers earlier in the day, and the entire massive lot of them were currently residing in the big walk-in cooler, waiting to be stripped and prepped. She'd get started on that tonight before heading home.

Someone knocked on the front door of the shop. She'd been closed for more than an hour. Thinking it might be Cayla with some last-minute wedding emergency, Misty went to answer. But it wasn't the slim blonde darkening her door. It was Denver.

Misty's heart leapt at the sight of him, but she hesitated near the register. She didn't know what to think or how to feel. Why was he here? Knowing he could see her in the dim light, she went ahead and opened the door.

"Can I come in?" His face was back to that stony expression that she knew now was the front he put on for everyone.

Misty stepped back to let him in, then locked the door behind him. "I'm working." Without waiting for a reply, she went on to the back, knowing he'd follow.

"The arbor is finished and set up over at the inn."

"Good. I need to get started tomorrow night."

As he came around the counter, Moxie leapt up from her bed and all but vaulted into his arms. He chuckled softly, scooping her up and scratching her behind the ears while she bathed his face in kisses. Impatient and ridiculously envious of her dog, Misty pulled the first batch of flowers from the cooler. Better to keep her hands busy. She spread them out on one of the tables and began the process of stripping lower leaves, ignoring Denver as he loved on Moxie.

Was this it? Was he just here to talk about the wedding or was he working his way up to something resembling an explanation?

"My father was diagnosed when I was twenty."

Whatever she'd expected him to say, it wasn't that. Her hands stilled on the flowers, but she didn't look at him.

"He was already stage three by the time they found it. Went in for something else, had some scans or whatever, and bam. Everything changed. We were suddenly charting food and meds and bathroom habits. He was still functional, could still do the job, but everything else revolved around keeping his kidneys functioning as long as possible. Then we ran into problems with his insurance. Probably the same kind of shit you dealt with. And while we were waiting for them to sort it out, he slid into stage four."

Misty's heart clenched. Because she knew this story. She'd dealt with this story so many times, with so many people. It was one of the core reasons why her job had been slowly sucking her soul away.

"That's when I started taking over stuff. He had a hard time concentrating. Wasn't sleeping for shit and hurting more often than not. And when the numbness hit his fingers, he couldn't do the work a lot of the time. He started losing out on jobs because he couldn't get them done fast enough. Some of them he just couldn't do, and I wasn't good enough yet.

He'd started dialysis, gotten on the transplant list. Things just kept getting worse. And the insurance company didn't give a good damn about it. He wasn't a person to them. Wasn't a face. He was just a name. A file. A string of eventually denied claims." Denver's voice was flat, but she could see the strain in his face as he spoke. She wanted nothing more than to wrap her arms around him, give him whatever comfort she could. But she didn't know if she'd be welcome, so she stayed quiet, listening, as he continued to stroke Moxie.

"I was twenty-five when they basically told us he'd maxed out his coverage. I spent so many hours on the phone arguing, trying to get him taken care of. He had a fucking chronic disease. What did they expect us to do? Nobody had an answer. And there wasn't someone like you on the other end even trying to find one." He lifted his gaze to hers. "I lost my father because the system is broken. And I despise them for it."

Misty thought she understood now. "And

telling you my story brought everything back for you."

He gave one short, sharp nod.

Regret sliced through her. He'd been so close to his dad. That had been obvious in nearly every conversation they'd had. She hated that she was a reminder of the worst parts of losing him. Hated, too, that the part of her life she'd tried to leave behind was tarnishing something she'd come to value so much.

Misty spread her hands. "I can't change my past, Denver."

"I wouldn't want you to. You aren't the system. You aren't the one who denied my father's claims. And I was an asshole for acting like you were."

Something in his tone let her know that he had more to say. "But?"

"No buts. I'm sorry for walking out on you when you were struggling. I'm sorry for shutting you out this week. And I'm sorry I didn't have the stones to just explain what was going through my head. You deserve better than that."

The *better than me* was implied.

Misty wanted to wrap her arms around him, offer some kind of comfort. But he still held Moxie and looked very much as if he wanted this conversation to be over. Maybe he needed all their conversations to be over. Even now, he didn't seem to quite be able to look at her. She wished, more than anything, that they could go back to last week, before she'd told him. But it would have come up eventually. And if this was a deal breaker for him, it was better to know now, before they got in any deeper.

"Thank you for telling me." What else could she say? If he still wanted a relationship with her, he had to say so. She wasn't going to force her company on him—wouldn't want to if that company came with a permanent reminder of his loss.

Denver's throat worked and he set Moxie

down. "I know you've got a lot of work to do. I'll let you get to it."

She wanted to stop him, to press for more. Instead, she followed him to the door. "I guess I'll see you at the wedding."

"Yeah." He glanced her way, just once, then slipped out the door and clearly out of her life.

CHAPTER 8

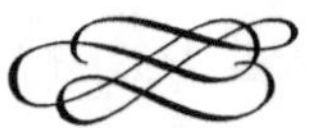

"I, Kennedy, take thee, Alexander, to be my husband—"

From several rows back, Denver bounced his leg. He was a man on a mission, and he just needed this ceremony over so he could get to it. He didn't know a lot about weddings, but he'd been sure that the florist's job was done once the flowers were dropped off. Apparently not. Despite the fact that he'd arrived early—with several gallons of his spiked lemonade for the reception—he hadn't managed five minutes to talk to Misty. He hadn't even managed to get close enough for five words.

When he'd left her at Moonbeams and Sweet Dreams the other night, he'd felt better having made his apologies. In telling her the truth, he'd finally been able to set aside the noxious emotional brew that had been eating at him for a week. But as he'd come home to Oscar, who'd stopped wagging almost as soon as he realized Moxie and Misty hadn't been with him, a whole different level of shitty had rolled in to fill that void. He missed Misty. He missed hanging out with her and the dogs. He missed talking over his day with her. He missed seeing what flowers she'd tucked into her hair every day. By wallowing in his old wounds, he'd cut her out and left a gaping hole in his life. That was when he realized he hadn't fixed shit. At least not all the way. He wanted her to give him another chance. He'd been all raring to go to follow through, but Misty had been busy with the wedding—

the last two days were her prime go time—so he'd had to wait.

Once he'd made up his mind about something, Denver hated waiting.

The woman in the next seat turned a fulminating glare on him. Denver stopped bouncing his knee and rubbed damp palms on his pants. They just had to get through the rest of the ceremony, then he could corner her during pictures. Except once the *I dos* were said and the bride was kissed, Misty disappeared and Denver got drafted to help quickly move all the tables at the perimeter and set up for the reception.

Where the hell did she go?

"Denver Hershal, I had no idea you were so talented!" Essie Vaughn, dispatcher and receptionist at the Sheriff's Office, stepped into his path. "That arbor is just beautiful."

"Thank you, Mrs. Vaughn."

"Where did you learn how to do that?"

"My dad taught me. He was a cabinetmaker and master carpenter." Denver scanned the crowds of people busily placing chairs around the moved tables.

"Such a wonderful skill to have. A dying art."

He worked up a smile because he wasn't a total dick. "Thanks, Mrs. Vaughn. If you'll excuse me, I need to go find Misty."

Essie beamed at him and tapped her nose. "Of course you do. Go right on ahead, honey."

Denver cut a swath through the other guests, making a beeline for outside. Maybe she'd gone up to the inn to help with food? He got waylaid again four more times by people offering praise or asking questions about the damned arbor. Xander's mama tried to talk him into building one out at their place. It took him another fifteen minutes to shake loose of her without being rude. It seemed prudent to make the effort since her son could arrest him. This. This was why he didn't do this for a living. His fuse was getting shorter by the minute. He needed to *find Misty*.

There! Denver spotted her across the barn, adjusting the centerpieces on each table.

Head down, he plowed through the crowd like the offensive lines he used to break in high school football. Misty's eyes widened as he made it to the table. As she'd known he'd be here, he could only imagine he looked pretty intense.

"I need to talk to you."

"Is something wrong?" she asked

Everything. "There are some things I need to say."

Misty frowned. "Here?"

"Yeah." Denver paused, aware of all the people milling about. "Well, not right on this spot. C'mon." He took her hand, relieved when she didn't protest as he pulled her out of the barn.

There were more people milling about, working on transferring food for the buffet, and the wedding party was taking pictures across the yard, but it wasn't wall-to-wall bodies. He kept going until he hit a bench on an overlook a little ways from the house, out of earshot and out of the line of the camera. He paused there, looking out over the mountains he'd made home, waiting for the peace they usually brought to seep into him. It didn't. Peace had eluded him from the day he'd walked away from her. If this didn't work…

It had to work.

He turned to Misty and tightened his grip on the hand he still held. It was daisies twined in her hair today. They were always his favorite. Something simple and cheerful that suited the sweet nature he'd come to crave. He wanted her back in his life as more than somebody to wave to on the street. He wanted everything he'd been too afraid to grab hold of. "I was wrong."

She shook her head, clearly not understanding. "Denver, you already apologized. We're good."

"No we're not. The apology was part of it, but after I finished prying my head out of my ass, I realized exactly how badly I screwed up. Because there's a you-sized hole in my life."

Misty stared at him.

Hell, he was still screwing this up. Impatient, he ran a hand over his hair. "I miss you. And Oscar may never forgive me if he doesn't get to see Moxie again. We want you back, if you can see your way to forgiving me for being a dumbass."

There. He'd said it. He'd put the whole thing out there. Now, heart in his throat, Denver held his breath, knowing it was out of his hands.

WE WANT YOU BACK.

He might have been slow, but he'd finally made a move. And it was exactly what Misty had wanted him to say the other night. But though her heart pounded with hope, with excitement, there was no little bit of fear mixed in. She'd let down her walls with this man.

She'd let him into her life further than any man in years, and at the first sign of trouble, he'd run. What guarantee did she have that he wouldn't do it again? That the memories she inadvertently evoked for him wouldn't get thrown back in her face somewhere down the line?

I was wrong.

Did he really mean it? He looked so penitent staring down at her with those clear gray eyes. A rare streak of vulnerability colored his expression, and Misty realized she had the capacity to hurt him, too. This big, intense, broody man was actually holding his breath, waiting for her to answer. Maybe that told her everything she needed to know.

"Having an emotional trauma and choosing to go off and deal with it on your own instead of taking it directly out on me does not make you a dumbass." Misty had worked her way around to that over the past couple of days. She wished he'd told her at the time, but she realized that, in his own way, he'd been trying to protect her from his reaction. "You could have been incredibly ugly to me over the whole thing. I know ugly. I've been used to being blamed for things that aren't my fault, that I had no actual control over. You didn't do that. My story brought up some big emotional stuff for you—stuff you usually keep locked away—and rather than unleash it on me unfairly, you went off to brood on your own. And yeah, that hurt me, so let's not do that ever again. But I can understand it. I even see a strength of character in how you handled yourself."

Denver ducked his head. Was he *blushing?* Sure enough, color was creeping up his neck. "Does that mean you'll give me another chance?"

He'd come this far on his own. She could meet him the rest of the way. Sliding her arms around his neck, Misty rose to her toes and brushed her lips against his. "We can't break the dogs' hearts, now can we?"

Denver's arms closed around her and

Misty found herself lifted off the ground as he spun her in a fast circle, before his mouth came down on hers for a kiss that meant serious business. It was the smattering of applause that brought Misty back to herself. Pulling back, she felt her own cheeks heat as she realized half the wedding guests had spilled out onto the lawn and were watching, as were the wedding party.

"Well. I guess they came for the wedding and got an extra show," she muttered.

"Don't mind us," Denver hollered. "I'm just kissing my girl."

The guests grinned. Across the yard, Misty spotted Cayla and Kennedy sharing a high five. Most of those who saw it probably thought they were congratulating themselves on the nigh flawless execution of a quick wedding. But as they both shot matching grins in her direction, she knew what it was really about. She was far too grateful to be annoyed.

Pivoting back into his arms, she arched both brows. "Your girl, huh?"

A flicker of doubt crossed his face. "Minus a week of me being pig-headed, I kinda thought we were headed in that direction."

"We were," she conceded. "But a girl likes to be asked."

Denver's smile spread like sun-warmed honey as he pulled her closer. "Misty Pennebaker, will you be my girlfriend?"

"I'd love to," she said, and lifted her lips to his.

EPILOGUE

As Denver leaned into the turn, Misty pressed close, her arms tightening around his waist. He loved feeling her snugged up against his back when they took Roxanne out for a ride. She'd taken to the motorcycle like a duck to water. He'd offered to teach her to ride on her own, but she preferred riding with him, and who was he to complain about any up-close-and-personal time of any kind with his girl? And on a day like today, when the sky stretched out in a ribbon of endless blue and the temperatures held the first hint of autumn, it was perfect.

Almost.

It would be up to her whether they made it all the way.

Denver found himself unaccountably nervous. Under the guise of reassuring her, he reached back to stroke a hand along the outside of her thigh. She squeezed him back. Releasing a breath, he forced himself to relax.

Things were great between them—had been great for four months—and he wanted to lock things in. He wanted this woman in his life for the everyday and always, and he didn't need any more time to think about taking the next big step. This was the right move, even if she wasn't gonna see it coming.

Taking the next fork in the road, he wound his way around to the opposite side of the valley, up into the hills just north of town. Sunlight filtered through the trees to dapple the road. It was a picture, one he committed to memory as he slowed the bike and pulled into a narrow lane. Behind him, Misty straightened, obviously wondering where he was taking her. She'd see soon enough.

They broke free of the trees into a wide clearing with a view to part of the valley. The house at the center had seen better days and was out of date by at least a couple of decades. But the gardens that stretched beyond it… those had seen love a lot more recently. Denver drove around to the back and parked with Roxanne pointed toward the stellar view.

Misty slid off in a smooth motion, already yanking off her helmet so her hair came tumbling down. "These gardens are gorgeous! Where are we?" Damn, she was a sight in her own leather jacket and those skinny jeans.

Denver took a moment to appreciate the view she made all on her own before dismounting and tugging off his own helmet. "I thought you might like them. The property belongs to the mom of a customer of mine. She spent her retirement building the gardens out. They were her pride and joy. Her son hired me to redo the cabinets a couple years back, and she used to love talking about them. She's a helluva gardener."

"I'll say." She took a couple of steps toward a row of rose bushes. "What are we doing here?"

"I thought you'd like to see the gardens. They seemed up your alley." That wasn't all, but it was the start to his plan.

"Should we knock and say hello?"

"She's not here anymore. She's been having some health problems the last few months and recently moved to be closer to her daughter in Kentucky."

"Oh, how sad. It's obvious she put a ton of work into them. It's tragic she had to leave them behind. I hope her son is willing to put in the work to keep them up."

So far, so good.

"Go ahead and take a look around."

Denver trailed after her as she moved from one bed to the next, identifying flowers and compulsively plucking weeds as she went.

"You ever want to actually garden? I know you've got your pots and stuff at home, but is that enough for you? Are you basically done with flowers after spending all day with them at work?" He was pretty sure the answer was no. She'd already added pots of this and that around his place. Bright spots of color and cool greenery that added a homey touch he hadn't known he'd been missing.

"I do the pot thing because I live in a rental. And because I had to spend so much time getting the shop up and going those first couple of years. But someday I'd *love* to have a showplace of a garden like this. Oh my God, look at these orchids! " She crouched down and brushed detritus away from some tender pink blooms.

Swallowing hard, Denver stuck his hands in his pockets to keep from rubbing them against his pants. He could be casual about this. "It's for sale."

"What?" Her tone was distracted, her attention still clearly on the flowers.

He tried again. "The property. It's for sale."

She straightened, looking back at the house. "It'd be a hell of an investment for somebody. The house needs work."

He pivoted to look it over himself, skimming his gaze from the roofline down. "It's got good bones. Needs some updates. Yank down those awnings and swap them for shutters. Swap those spindly columns for some solid cedar beams. Update the paint. The interior's a bit dated, but nothing too much more than cosmetic. There are hardwoods under the carpet, and the bathrooms got updated the same year as the kitchen cabinets. Cindy had a helluva gardening shed over there off the garage, and there's easy room to set up a woodshop. We'd need to fence off part of the yard for the dogs, but that's easily accomplished."

When he looked back at Misty, she wasn't looking at the house anymore. She was staring at him. "What are you saying?"

I want more. I want you. "I think we should move in together."

"Here?"

She'd jumped straight to logistics. That was a good sign, right? Or maybe she was just stuck on pure disbelief.

"I mean, we don't have to, if you don't like it. But your place doesn't have room for my workshop. My place doesn't have easy room for all your stuff. This property would suit all our needs and still have plenty of room for us to customize." Stepping toward her, he grasped her hands, hoping she didn't notice his sweaty palms. "I wanna build something with you, and I think this place has tons of potential."

"You want to move in together?"

Why did she still look so surprised? "I mean…yeah. Didn't I say that?"

"That's a big step. It's only been four months."

Was that the issue? He couldn't blame her skepticism. He'd been the one to let her take the lead almost their entire relationship. But he was more than ready to take this next step.

"I don't need to wait when I finally figure out what I want, and I want you, Misty. Morning, noon, and night. If you don't like this property, we'll find another one together. But say you'll build something with me."

Her big brown eyes glimmered with emotion. "You're really sure?"

"Really, really. This is right. *We're* right." And wasn't it a wonder, to have that certainty? "You're the brightness I've been missing in my life, and I don't ever want to go back to the dark. I love you. I probably should've led with that."

Her face melted into a broad smile and she rose up to her toes, pressing her cheek to his. "I love you, too. God, so much."

The sweetness of that swept through him, wiping out the nerves and the worry that he'd moved too fast, for once in his life. No matter what she said next, he'd have that. He could wait for the rest, if he had to.

Misty linked her arms behind his neck and tipped back her head to look into his eyes, hers full of everything he'd hoped to see. "I'd love to build something with you, Denver. I'd even love to build it here."

Relief and excitement had him snaking his arms around her waist to haul her close, brushing his mouth to hers. "That's good to hear because I already made an offer."

Misty pulled back on a laugh, beaming a smile. "You did what?"

He shrugged. "Steve let me have first bid. If you didn't like it, he'd have just put it on the market like normal, but he was happy to let me have first crack at it. The place is ours, if we want it."

She melted against him. "I want it. I want you. I want us. So yeah, let's do it."

And that was the perfect beginning to the perfect rest of his life.

CHOOSE YOUR NEXT ROMANCE

I HOPE you enjoyed this opposites attract romance! The Misfit Inn journey continues with *Those Sweet Words,* Pru and Flynn's story, which overlaps with this one during Kennedy's wedding. There's a wedding fling and a fake engagement that you won't want to miss! If this was your first visit to The Misfit Inn, the series begins with *When You Got A Good Thing,* Kennedy and Xander's story.

If you're digging more opposites attract romance, have some one with a side of sexy former Army Ranger and another Reynolds family wedding (that'll be Athena's wedding, in case you want to read her book *Stay A Little Longer* first), check out *What I Like About You!*

OTHER BOOKS BY KAIT NOLAN

A complete and up-to-date list of all my books can be found at https://kaitnolan.com.

THE MISFIT INN SERIES
SMALL TOWN FAMILY ROMANCE

- *When You Got A Good Thing* (Kennedy and Xander)

- *Til There Was You* (Misty and Denver)
- *Those Sweet Words* (Pru and Flynn)
- *Stay A Little Longer* (Athena and Logan)
- *Bring It On Home* (Maggie and Porter)

RESCUE MY HEART SERIES
SMALL TOWN MILITARY ROMANCE

- *Baby It's Cold Outside* (Ivy and Harrison)
- *What I Like About You* (Laurel and Sebastian)
- *Bad Case of Loving You* (Paisley and Ty prequel)
- *Made For Loving You* (Paisley and Ty)

MEN OF THE MISFIT INN
SMALL TOWN SOUTHERN ROMANCE

- *Let It Be Me* (Emerson and Caleb)

- *Our Kind of Love* (Abbey and Kyle)
- *Don't You Wanna Stay* (Deanna and Wyatt)
- *Come A Little Closer* (Samantha and Griffin)

Wishful Series
Small Town Southern Romance

- *Once Upon A Coffee* (Avery and Dillon)
- *To Get Me To You* (Cam and Norah)
- *Know Me Well* (Liam and Riley)
- *Be Careful, It's My Heart* (Brody and Tyler)
- *Just For This Moment* (Myles and Piper)
- *Wish I Might* (Reed and Cecily)
- *Turn My World Around* (Tucker and Corinne)
- *Dance Me A Dream* (Jace and Tara)
- *See You Again* (Trey and Sandy)

- *The Christmas Fountain* (Chad and Mary Alice)
- *You Were Meant For Me* (Mitch and Tess)
- *A Lot Like Christmas* (Ryan and Hannah)
- *Dancing Away With My Heart* (Zach and Lexi)

WISHING FOR A HERO SERIES (A WISHFUL SPINOFF SERIES)
SMALL TOWN ROMANTIC SUSPENSE

- *Make You Feel My Love* (Judd and Autumn)
- *Watch Over Me* (Nash and Rowan)
- *Can't Take My Eyes Off You* (Ethan and Miranda)
- *Burn For You* (Sean and Delaney)

MEET CUTE ROMANCE
SMALL TOWN SHORT ROMANCE

- *Once Upon A Snow Day*
- *Once Upon A New Year's Eve*
- *Once Upon An Heirloom*
- *Once Upon A Coffee*
- *Once Upon A Campfire*
- *Once Upon A Rescue*

SUMMER CAMP
CONTEMPORARY ROMANCE

- *Once Upon A Campfire*
- *Second Chance Summer*

ABOUT KAIT

Kait is a Mississippi native, who often swears like a sailor, calls everyone sugar, honey, or darlin', and can wield a bless your heart like a saber or a Snuggie, depending on requirements.

You can find more information on this RITA ® Award-winning author and her books on her website http://kaitnolan.com.

Do you need more small town sass and spark? Sign up for her newsletter to hear about new releases, book deals, and exclusive content!

www.ingramcontent.com/pod-product-compliance
Lightning Source LLC
Chambersburg PA
CBHW070548100726
47907CB00004B/1309